The Sky Is Crying

Galactic Blues Book 3

by

D.L. Martone

For Lindsay Buroker,

the most inspiring sci-fi and fantasy author we know

Chapter
1

REMY

"AHHHHHHHH," Captain Remy Bechet shouted as the escape descender hit the planet's atmosphere.

After getting propelled into space, via the ass end of a pneumatic tube, he'd initially experienced the free-floating weightlessness of zero-g, but now, his body trembled from the extreme, bone-shaking effects of Voxian gravity, and his headache predictably raged with a vengeance.

"Th-thisss i-iss aaaa d-d-death-tr-trappp," he stuttered to himself.

No one could hear him scream, of course. As far as he knew, the capsule contained no mics or speakers, but the sound of his voice—admittedly difficult to discern amid the rattles and clunks of the vibrating ship—distracted him from more morose thoughts. Such as the real possibility that he was about to splat like a freaking pancake on the arid terrain outside Trame—especially since the heavy-duty sedative coursing through his bloodstream might make it tough for him to manually activate the parachute.

He didn't fancy dying like that—no matter how quick and painless it might prove to be—and he certainly didn't want poor Drey to see him in such a goopy, unrecognizable state.

Crap. Dreyla.

In his haste to return to Trame, he'd forgotten to contact the monastery and warn them of his imminent arrival. Hopefully, Georgia or Zia had thought to do that in his stead.

The ship shook even more, and the unnerving rattles loudened. Suddenly, the jarring experience reminded him of his childhood on Earth, when he'd eagerly paid for amusement-park rides designed to make kids holler and vomit.

This quivering descender was an extreme version of those—but with a higher mortality rate.

The pod quaked more violently, and flames jumped alongside the portholes. Remy's queasy stomach leapt toward his throat, the veins and arteries in his cranium threatened to explode, and his vision narrowed considerably, the peripheral edges as pitch-black as space.

Wait. Did *Zia give me a sedative, or did I imagine that?*

He could feel a sore spot on his neck, but still... shouldn't the damn drug have kicked in by now?

Although he normally preferred having a lucid mind, able to spot trouble coming from a mile away, a part of him wished he'd been completely knocked out before embarking on this one-way trip to oblivion. At least he wouldn't have to hear his teeth chattering or feel his organs threatening to burst through his skin.

Escape pod. Descent vehicle. Deceptively innocent names for a human-sized bullet aimed directly at a planet's surface.

Oh, yeah. This was a stellar idea.

The capsule's vibrations worsened, unleashing even more aches and pains throughout his body. Not just the ones in his skull.

"AHHHHHHHH," he yelled again, thankful that those on the ground couldn't witness him screaming like an unhinged toddler.

Drey and Tosh would've mocked him for years to come.

Drey. Tosh.

Reflecting on the two of them, Remy promised himself—yet again—that he would fly them off this stupid planet and back to their own galaxy. A galaxy where Tosh was a merciful emperor and Dreyla could soar like a butterfly.

Wait, what?

Was that right? Could Dreyla really glide like a big, beautiful butterfly? She was pretty graceful when she chose to be. And was Tosh actually a galactic emperor back home? The much-beloved ruler of all that was trippy?

Whoa. What's happening to me?

His thoughts made no sense... or did they? Maybe he was seeing the truth for the first time ever.

Sure, why not?

But who was Remy back home? And better yet, where was he right now?

He slowly pivoted his head toward one of the portholes. Radiant streams of orange and yellow erupted and then vanished, and all at once, the tremors lessened, and he was floating again. Maybe he and his daughter were both giant butterflies, wearing mere human disguises.

Must be true... cuz here I am floating through the air.

Then, even that came to an abrupt halt.

Chapter 2

DREYLA

Dreyla Bechet peered inside the capsule and squinted. "Are you stoned?"

Remy lay on his side in the overturned vessel, still strapped into his seat. Even through the helmet he wore, she could see his own slit-eyed gaze staring back at her. Less likely from curiosity and suspicion and more likely due to the blinding sunlight pouring into the pod.

While the captain had been making his death-defying plummet back to Vox, Georgia had warned the monastery that he was on his way. When asked about his condition, she'd admitted that, despite his potential head trauma, he was too stubborn to delay—a fact that Drey understood all too well. At the very least, they'd decided to give him a powerful sedative to lower his blood pressure.

But Drey didn't require the heads-up. Remy's goofy grin made it clear he was high on something—not a common occurrence for him.

Although the parachute had deployed on time and guided him safely to the ground, he'd apparently been too loopy to press the button that would open the hatch. So, Lady Ris had had to bust into the pod the old-fashioned way: with a crowbar. OK, it was actually a pneumatic separator, but it certainly resembled a crowbar.

Luckily, Remy seemed intact, if not quite himself.

Tosh knelt beside Dreyla and chuckled. "Way to go, Captain. Where'd you score the junk?"

Drey sighed. Typical Tosh. If they weren't dealing with an emergency, he was usually thinking about where he'd score his next hit of dope.

Well, that and sex. He's an odd ol' bird, but I still love him.

All kidding aside, though, Dreyla had never witnessed Remy in his current state. She'd seen him under anesthesia before—many times, in fact—but never quite like this.

She crawled inside the pod and carefully removed his helmet.

He lolled his head toward her, his eyes languid and moony. "Hey, Drey. Where are your wings?"

"Man," Tosh said as he unbuckled the captain's restraints, "that must've been some amazing dope they gave you."

"Just a sedative to lower his blood pressure," Lady Ris clarified from outside the pod. "If he sustained a head injury in the collision, my ladies would have been concerned about the negative effects of him dropping."

"Makes sense," Doc said. "But still, I've pumped a lot of stuff into this man over the years. Never reacted like that before."

Gingerly, he and Drey pulled Remy from the pod. Back on his feet again, the captain wobbled a bit and spun around in place, gazing dreamily at the surrounding area.

"Must be having a bad reaction to it," Dreyla observed.

"Bad? Nah, he's having a fantastic ride." Tosh grinned from ear to ear. "Ground control to Major Bechet."

Dreyla flashed him a stern look. "Doc, this isn't funny..."

He winked at her, gently stopped Remy from spinning, and removed a slender injection gun from his pocket. Then, without preamble, he pressed the needle into the captain's neck and pushed the release button.

In a flash, Remy's eyes brightened. "What the hell?"

Tosh patted his shoulder. "Welcome back, Captain."

"Well, that was different," he mumbled.

Before he could elaborate, however, Dreyla pressed herself against him and threw her arms around his torso. He immediately embraced her in return.

She sniffed, her eyes watering. "Thought I'd lost you."

"Pshaw." He squeezed her harder. "Come on, kid. Takes a lot more than that to kill me."

No matter what he said, the tears kept rolling down her cheeks. She felt as if she were eight years old again, but she didn't care.

"Hey, Drey," Remy said, trying to console her, "I promise you, you're not gonna lose me... at least not anytime soon."

"Promise?"

"I promise."

She nodded, sniffed, and then pulled away slightly to punch him in the shoulder.

"Ow." Remy squirmed out of her arms. "What the hell was that for?"

"Just cuz." She wiped her face. "You scared me."

Remy opened his mouth to retort, but he didn't get

the chance.

"Hate to break up this tender reunion," Lilly said, "but I think we'd better get back to the plan."

Obviously startled, Remy stiffened as he turned toward the voice. He must not have realized how many people had converged upon the crash site.

Despite her annoyance with the sheriff, Dreyla couldn't help but giggle. She knew how much the big tough pirate hated getting emotional in public.

"You know," Lilly prodded, "the little matter of stealing our meds back."

Remy quickly recovered. "I'm well aware of the plan, Sheriff. Why do you think I insisted on getting back down here so fast?" He nodded toward the pod. "In fact, you'll find the monastery's reserves inside."

While two monks crawled into the capsule to retrieve the nano-biotics, Dreyla scanned the faces of those around her. In the harsh light of the Voxian sun, she could clearly read the concern in their eyes. Lady Ris and her ladies, Sheriff Greyson and her deputies, the dworg, the aflin... all of them were worried about the health—and survival—of their people.

She sympathized with them, of course, but mostly, she was just grateful to have her father back.

Remy winked at her. "OK, let's get this done."

Dreyla frowned. "You sure? You've whacked your

head at least twice this week. How many concussions can you take?"

He winced. "Just a headache. No biggie."

"Hang on, Captain," Tosh cautioned. "I should check you out first. In case it's worse than you think."

"You're the boss, Doc." Remy flashed his roguish grin. "But then we get this show on the road. OK?"

With an agreeable nod, Tosh led him toward the open gates of the monastery. Dreyla sighed as she trailed behind the two men.

What they intended to do to reclaim the planet's nans wouldn't be easy. Frankly, nothing ever was.

Chapter 3

LILLY

The brisk, hot breeze whipped Sheriff Lilly Greyson's ponytail as the hovercraft glided above the desert. This was it—they were on their way to Bane. Not far ahead, another hovercraft, occupied by two radiant monks and three large trunks, led the way. The containers held Davis, Milo, and Jacer, none of whom had been pleased with this part of the plan.

Following in the lead vehicle's tailwind and driven by Lady Ris herself, the second hovercraft carried another gorgeous monk, appropriately called Bellia, plus Lilly,

Dreyla, and Brand, all of whom wore the customary garb of the Ladies of Morbious. Behind Lilly and her cohorts sat yet another trunk, this one concealing a rather disgruntled Bechet.

As much as Lilly might have preferred to stay in Trame for a few more days, helping the Ladies of Morbious with repairs and relaxing amid the normally tranquil, paradisal ambience of the monastery, it felt good to be on the move again. For a fleeting moment, she'd relished the peaceful familiarity of the monks' desert oasis, but last night's battle had yanked her back to reality, reminding her of what typically constituted the life of Naillik's sheriff: adversity, danger, and death.

Doing her best to tip the scales of justice against the weight of evil men (and women) was the closest Lilly had gotten to embracing a sense of purpose.

But am I prepared to die to get those meds back?

A loud bang erupted from the nearby cargo trunk, startling Lilly from her meandering thoughts.

"It ain't easy to breathe in here," came Bechet's muffled voice. "Geez, we better be getting close."

Lilly turned toward the container and rapped her knuckles atop the lid. "Shut up, Bechet, or you'll end up with one of Darkbur's men shooting a hole in that dashing

13

head of yours."

Dreyla giggled. Despite the obvious tension between her and Lilly, the girl had elected to sit beside her on the journey to Bane. Clearly, she felt self-conscious about her revealing costume. Lilly understood her discomfort and, to a certain degree, shared it, but Dreyla had demanded to join the mission, so she couldn't have it both ways.

"I heard that, Drey," Bechet's voice rumbled from the trunk.

The girl's grin widened further.

"We could have placed them inside the trunks much closer to Bane," Bellia whispered. "There was no need for them to ride the whole way like that."

"You never know when you'll cross paths with a patrol or a caravan." Not wanting to tempt fate, Lilly picked up her long-range binoculars to scan the terrain again. "Besides, it's so much nicer with the menfolk put in their proper place."

"And I heard that, too," Remy grumbled from the trunk.

"What excellent hearing you have, Captain," she said. "For someone who doesn't like to listen."

The leading hovercraft decelerated as the city of Bane grew closer. Lady Ris pulled her vehicle alongside it and then eased into the front position.

"It is kinda pleasant not having them around," Brand mused, patting some structure back into her blonde hair.

Dreyla's eyes widened. She obviously hadn't expected her to say that. Perhaps she'd also noticed the flirtations between Brand and Davis.

Brand winked at the youngster. "Sometimes, men can be such a pain in the ass. You'll soon find out."

"But they can also be a great source of pleasure," Lady Ris replied from the driver's seat with a benevolent smile.

Brand blushed.

Dreyla and Lilly chuckled, the latter wondering if trouble was brewing between her newest deputy and the currently boxed-up Davis.

Well, tough.

If they both survived this caper, they could mangle each other then.

"I am sorry we could not carry more gear into the city," Lady Ris continued, turning back to focus on driving.

"No worries." Lilly stowed the binoculars under her seat. "The guards at the city gates need to see exactly what they expect to see from you all." She gritted her teeth. "Everything has to look real normal."

Lady Ris scrutinized Lilly's face in the rear-view mirror, as if sensing the doubt and trepidation she'd valiantly attempted to conceal.

"We will be able to smuggle in more of your gear later," Lady Ris assured her, "but Bane is quite specific about what kind of crafts and how much cargo can enter at any given time."

"Of course," Lilly reasoned. "Darkbur's trying to ensure that none of the other organizations can bring in anything that could upset the balance of power."

Lady Ris nodded. "Yes, well, we will haul the rest in tomorrow, with another wave of the Ladies of Morbious. Everything your captain wanted."

"He's not *my* captain," Lilly blurted, and then instantly regretted it.

Dreyla's lips curled into a smile that suggested a private victory.

From the start of this weeklong mess, the girl had staunchly defended her captain, which made sense given their father-daughter vibe. Despite their obvious physical differences—his light skin and hazel eyes, her dark complexion and even darker eyes—they seemed to share a lot of expressions and personality quirks, from shrewd intelligence to stubborn indignation. Even if Bechet wasn't Dreyla's biological father, she obviously considered him a surrogate one.

So, Lilly's harsh treatment of him had naturally elicited a wave of teenaged angst from the girl—plus a certain amount of glee whenever Lilly demonstrated how much Bechet rankled her. Dreyla's emotions weren't those of a simple crew member. No, these two shared an unusually close bond.

Lady Ris guided the hovercraft behind others waiting to enter the city. The line was long, but the guards at the gates typically kept the entrants moving at an efficient rate.

Lilly had traveled to Bane a few times before—primarily to help Jett Cansen, Naillik's mayor, negotiate various mining rights—so she knew what to expect. It amused her that they'd always held those meetings with Bane's mayor, Hansen Timms, who possessed no real power. Just a puppet, with Gono Darkbur pulling all his strings.

"Damn," Lady Ris exclaimed.

"What is it?" Anxiety bloomed in Lilly's gut. She'd never heard her spiritual mentor use an expletive before.

Even in the wake of Darkbur's unprecedented siege on the monastery, Lady Ris had remained her regal, even-tempered self.

But perhaps her frustrated tone shouldn't have surprised Lilly. She knew Lady Ris well enough to sense the seething anger behind her composed visage. The head monk had already wanted to assist their mission for the

17

sake of all the Voxians in need of the life-saving nans. Now, however, she had a new reason to join the fight: to avenge the lives of her fallen sisters and seek restitution for her besmirched home.

Lady Ris peered at the control screen of her hover-craft. Lilly leaned forward to snatch her own glimpse of the display and realized the head monk had been running long-range surveillance on the approaching gates. Unfortunately, the sensors had spotted a troubling addition to Bane's usual security measures: The guards were now scanning every face that entered the city.

Damn, indeed.

"You," Lady Ris said, turning to Brand, her green eyes flashing, "head to the other craft and conceal yourself in one of the trunks."

The deputy hesitated, glancing nervously between the monk and her boss.

"Go," Lady Ris yelled. "And take Dreyla with you!"

"Dammit," Lilly growled, realizing that Bane's security personnel could have easily nabbed photos of her newest recruit and the incarcerated juvenile. "Brand, Dreyla, hurry! Tell the others what's going on."

The two of them hopped out of the slow-moving hovercraft, dashed across the sand, and clambered inside the second vehicle. Lilly could only hope that, if Brand opted to hide inside Davis's container, her two deputies would keep their hands off each other and their minds focused on the mission.

"You, too, Lilly," Lady Ris urged, snapping her out of her inconvenient musings.

Reluctantly, Lilly gazed down at Bechet's trunk. Although she didn't want to admit it, she knew that Lady Ris was right. Even without the facial-recognition software, the guards might figure out her identity and bust apart their scheme before it had even commenced.

Frankly, she should have suspected such a wrinkle in the plan. Perhaps she would have, too, had she not lost so much sleep to last night's siege. Now, Lilly regretted the oversight. She, Dreyla, and Brand could have forgone the flimsy costumes and hidden inside the trunks from the start.

Still, she couldn't imagine sharing such a cramped space with the irritating pirate.

"Come on in," Bechet said, as if reading her thoughts. "There's plenty of room."

Though muffled, his voice sounded decidedly amused.

With a resigned sigh, Lilly slowly opened the container. The top compartment held a combination of recruitment materials and medical supplies, innocuous items that the Ladies of Morbious normally carted into Bane. She lifted the false bottom and spotted Bechet in the hollow space beneath. Presently, he lay on his side, with his torso corkscrewed upward, his head cradled atop his folded arms, and a huge, self-satisfied grin on his face.

He scooted to one side, leaving almost half the space empty. "See? Plenty of room."

No words came to mind. She simply shook her head and, avoiding the stares of her companions, gingerly stepped one foot inside and then the other. Once she was settled beside Bechet, Bellia replaced the false bottom, and the lid clicked shut above them.

The sudden darkness made Lilly's breath hitch. She'd never suffered from claustrophobia, but she still wasn't fond of tight spaces. Besides, it already felt stuffy in here, and a whole plethora of disaster scenarios flooded her mind, all leading to her inevitable demise.

Just breathe. Keep calm.

Once Lilly subdued her panic, she felt another sensation roiling within her chest. She squirmed against the nearest wall as best she could, but nothing could help her cope with the fact that she lay in a snug, private space with a breathing, pulsing, strangely intoxicating male. Their bodies were pressed so tightly against one another that she could feel almost every inch of the man.

Even in the pitch-black space, she knew Bechet was enjoying their proximity way too much.

"Stop smiling," she demanded.

"How could you possibly know I'm smiling?" he asked.

"I can hear it."

He chuckled.

She jabbed her elbow into his chest.

"Oomph," he said.

Sorry, not sorry.

Then, to her horror, she sensed something poking into the soft flesh of her thigh. "That better not be what I think it is," she hissed.

"Relax, Sheriff, it's just my gun," came his low husky voice, his breath tickling her ear.

That's no freaking gun.

She clenched her eyes shut and prayed for swift progress through this nightmare. Parts of her that had lain dormant for a long time had started to pulsate into life, which made lying still and rigid even more agitating. Even the steady rise and fall of Bechet's chest affected her. She couldn't turn off this hyper-awareness of him.

Outside the trunk, a sudden stillness descended. The hovercraft had probably stopped at the gates. She felt Bechet's muscles tense in concert with her own. Their shallow breaths coordinated as they strained to hear what the guards were saying to Lady Ris.

When the hovercraft started up again, she almost sunk against Bechet in relief, but she wouldn't make it that easy for him.

Five minutes later, they were coursing at a decent speed through Bane. The noise level rose severely. Even through the sturdy container, she could hear the unrelenting din of shouts, cheers, and confrontations.

Another five minutes passed, the vehicle came to a halt, and Lilly could feel their trunk rise and shift. It swayed with the rhythmic movement of pallbearers, periodically forcing her and her companion to roll against each other.

Lilly noted that, like her, Remy had grown quiet. Although his "gun" was still talking.

After what seemed like an eternity, someone opened the lid and removed the false bottom. Blinding indoor light and relatively fresh air rushed in, and she and Bechet both sucked in long breaths of relief.

"You first," he said.

Lilly grabbed the edge of the trunk and clambered

out awkwardly. She hastily stepped away from her temporary prison and, unable to hold eye contact with her fellow prisoner, busied herself with straightening her bikini and robe.

"Another minute, and I was gonna pass out," Bechet said, his voice somewhat hoarse. He glanced around sharply.

"What's the problem?" she asked.

"How did they carry us in here?"

In here was the interior of a modest hotel bedroom with gray and red decor. The others were also present, either emerging from their trunks or stretching out their cramped muscles.

"Holy crap, Captain!" Dreyla rushed up to him. "It only took two of the Ladies of Morbious to carry you and the sheriff in."

Bechet glanced at the monks in question, who loitered in the doorway, talking in hushed tones. He scanned their willowy limbs, but not, oddly enough, with lust. His look was one of sheer approval.

So, strong women don't intimidate him.

"OK, Drey," he said, "you, the sheriff, and Deputy Brand will change into your civvies, and as soon as it's night, you'll scout the most likely area first. Around the...

Butcher's Place?"

His gaze caught Lilly's for the first time since their awkward trunk experience.

She nodded. Normally, she hated when men stepped on her toes, but his orders weren't meant to usurp her authority. He merely wanted to get this plan under-way—almost as much as she did.

"Butcher's Place," he repeated, grimacing. "Wonder how ol' Gono came up with that."

Chapter 4

DREYLA

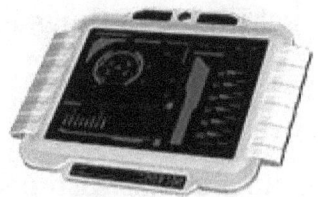

"Whoa, big guy," Dreyla said, keeping her voice low and steady. "I think we got off on the wrong foot."

The large man, pointing what seemed like an even larger blaster at her forehead, glanced downward and noticed her blade pressed ever so slightly against his crotch.

She arched one eyebrow, relishing his sharp intake of breath.

Off to the side, Sheriff Greyson frowned. With the tension escalating, she'd reached for her hip holster, but before she could draw her weapon, another man had crept up behind her with his gun drawn. He, in turn, had Deputy Brand's pistol pointed at his head, and Brand herself was now the target of a third man's weapon.

A classic stalemate. Or rather, a chain of disasters waiting to be triggered.

Dreyla had *told* the sheriff it was a bad idea to con-spicuously seek out information about the nano-biotics, but as usual, the "adults" hadn't listened. And now, here she and her two cohorts stood, locked in a standoff with three intimidating yet brainless thugs in a greasy, debris-filled alley.

Yet another reason she loved the captain: Even when in a disagreeable mood, he listened—to everybody—and then made what he considered the best decision. True, his brain didn't typically process information as everyone else's did, which was why he and his crew often ended up taking the not-so-smart path. Still, he did keep an open mind.

Would he listen, though, if Dreyla warned him about his infatuation with the sheriff? With that pretty face? That curvy figure? Nah, men were stupid.

Like this dude. His ugly face was getting dumber by the second. He was about to do something rash.

"Easy," Sheriff Greyson said. "Everybody, just calm down."

"And I said... drop yo' weapons," the thug holding

his gun against the sheriff's head growled in an equally authoritative tone.

Dreyla's assailant glanced away for a second, giving her an opening. Without hesitation, she slid around him, pushed his gun hand downward, and twisted it behind him. She ended up with her back against the concrete wall of a nearby building and her blade at the man's throat.

Luckily, his weapon hadn't gone off in the process, as it might've alerted curious passersby—although in the craphole that was Bane, she'd already heard numerous rounds of gunfire. So, perhaps it wouldn't have mattered.

"You little bitch," the man spat.

Her sly move had snagged everyone's attention. The other two thugs blinked rapidly, darting glances at each other. Deputy Brand's mouth fell agape, while the sheriff, with a half-smile on her face, just offered Dreyla a tiny nod of approval.

Still holding her blade against the thug's neck, Dreyla cleared her throat. "Do what the lady said... and calm down."

Sheriff Greyson carefully removed her hand from her holstered pistol and brought it up to her jacket, keeping her fingers visible. "I don't know who you all think we are," she said, her voice still admirably calm.

"We been told to keep an eye out for anyone we's don't know, askin' 'bout nans," the thug behind the sheriff snarled, jiggling his gun for emphasis.

"We're just here to do a little business." Sheriff Greyson cautiously turned her head to catch the apparent ringleader's eye. "Look, I'm going to reach into my jacket... slowly... and show you."

The woman was steady, Dreyla had to give her credit for that. Unlike poor Deputy Brand, whose sweat dribbled down her forehead, her blonde hair hanging limp against her pale cheeks. Her reaction only confirmed Dreyla's suspicion that she was one of the sheriff's newest deputies.

Well, nothing like a trial by fire.

Dreyla knew a thing or two about that kind of education. Story of her life.

Sheriff Greyson pulled out several packets of fake nano-biotics and extended them toward the man behind her. In a flash, he grabbed them and inspected the packaging, which required him to shift his undivided focus from his target. Perhaps the deadlock was finally easing up.

"These ain't got the scanner stamps." He flapped the packages under the sheriff's nose.

"Precisely. We've got a shipment of counterfeit meds we'd like to unload in the market."

Shaking his head, the man slowly lowered his gun.

"Mr. Darkbur says no more fake nans allowed, seeing as he's got the real thing over at the Butcher's."

He motioned for the man with the gun pointed at Deputy Brand to lower his weapon. He then shot a disgusted look at the other one, the one who'd allowed Dreyla to outwit him.

Sensing the situation was finally under control, Dreyla lowered her blade and stepped out from behind her quarry. Suddenly, the thug caught her face with a backhand, propelling her into the wall.

The painful blow of smashing against the concrete just compounded the insult.

She blinked her stinging eyes, her vision watery and blurry. She couldn't decide whether her face or her skull ached more. Both throbbed with pain, and she tasted blood on her lips.

The sheriff had drawn her pistol and pointed it at the thug's face. Brand's gun had swung to the same man. And the man that had previously held the sheriff at gunpoint had returned to the same position as before.

Oh, great. Right back where we started.

"OK, now yous all ease down," the thug leader said. "Georgie here's just pissed the *little girl* got the jump on him."

Dreyla dabbed the blood dripping from her nose and slowly righted herself. Once again, everyone lowered their weapons. Sheriff Greyson shot her a sympathetic look. Dreyla shrugged. Sadly, it wasn't the first time a dirtbag had caught her off-guard with a backhand. Of course, usually the guy in question soon felt her blades gliding across his legs and stomach, but this wasn't the time for those kinds of moves. They'd only make the situation worse.

"Yous can take yo' trash and unload it in Naillik or the other towns... just not here," the leader said. With a glare of disgust, he slapped the packs back into Sheriff Greyson's outstretched hand and motioned for his men to move out.

The three men withdrew from the alley and strutted onto the street, probably to harass someone else. Dreyla and her two companions breathed a sigh of relief, then Sheriff Greyson handed her a medical wipe she'd produced from her jacket pocket.

"Thanks, Sheriff."

The woman smiled. "Just Lilly."

Dreyla shrugged again and dabbed at the blood on her face, wondering how crappy she looked. Remy would certainly have a fit when he saw her. Still, it was a small price to pay for some helpful info.

As if reading her mind, Lilly said, "So, at least we

know for sure where Darkbur's keeping the nans."

Brand, whose natural color had returned, crinkled her brow. "What I don't get is why Darkbur's not advertising that he's got the meds. I would've figured word would be out by now, and people would be lining up to get them."

"He's probably only selling them to rich scumbags," Dreyla said. "Those he knows will pay premium." Having dealt with scum like these guys before, she pretty much knew the score.

"I'd say you're right," Lilly agreed. "He's cashing in, and then once the seriously rich have gotten their meds, he's going to hold the rest hostage in exchange for control of the planet."

The trio grew quiet. This was one massively screwed-up situation.

"How can he possibly think that would fly?" Dreyla asked hotly. "If there are a bunch of other planets out there, he's gotta know reinforcements will come."

Lilly sighed. "They're months away, and by that time, he'll own every inch of Vox." Her eyes lost focus for a moment.

"You all don't have any resources closer?" Dreyla asked.

"As Lady Ris said, there are several small space stations orbiting the planet, but that includes a rather well-armed one that represents Bane," Lilly replied.

The sheriff... Lilly... looked a bit lost. She had a crapstorm of trouble to deal with, and obviously, the fact that she needed the captain's help meant that she and her deputies were under-resourced.

Lilly straightened her posture and shook her head. "Come on, look sharp, let's get back to the others. We need to tell them what we found out."

Chapter 5

SHAW

"No, Commander, it's like a low-grade version of our TZ107," Zain said, offering her the measuring device.

Commander Tara Shaw scanned the readouts from Zain's Vox7 tests. The combustion efficiency figures promised a much lower magnitude than she would have expected.

"So, that's why their ships seem so underpowered."

Zain nodded. "The Vox7 provides them with a good source of energy, but it can't access the dark-matter streams and therefore can't draw from them."

"You're saying we're *stuck* on this planet?" Jibs whined.

Shaw turned to her sallow-faced second officer. "Calm down, Jibs. We don't need to go that far, or even that fast, to get the hell out of here. We just need to find that portal. It'll get us back to our solar system, where we can look for a better ride."

She'd made the plan sound so simple, but what were the chances of it working out? Most of the portals were temperamental, weren't they? Entropy and randomness wouldn't grind to a halt just because she desperately needed them to. Even if they did manage to procure a ship, and they found a portal somewhere near the orbit of this planet, they could conceivably find themselves traveling to a whole new universe, not their own.

Still, if anyone could get them back into space, Zain could. As for Jibs, she'd take him along for the ride, just in case she needed any dirty work done on the way. Plus, the two men seemed to be operating well together, despite their current circumstances and vast differences, so why break up the partnership?

"It's our best plan," Zain said, reclaiming his device and clicking off the display.

The young man was keeping up a brave face—probably for his colleague's sake. Jibs did seem a bit gloomy, after all. But surely, her first officer had also pondered the impossibility of their situation and reached his own ever-logical conclusion?

As if reading her mind, he winced. "The problem is, there aren't that many ships capable of breaking orbit. At least, not here in Bane."

"Yes, but how many, and how well guarded?" she demanded.

Her patience was frayed. She had left the task of formulating an escape plan to her two officers while she dealt with Darkbur, but none of them had gotten terribly far with either endeavor.

Hopefully, the Darkbur problem would resolve itself more quickly.

Though Darius had dismissed some of her suggestions, he'd at least agreed to run facial rec at the gates into Bane. She'd also managed to persuade him that searching for an entire crew (who might or might not be involved in any attempted recovery effort) would slow down entry too much. It was enough to keep a lookout for the sheriff and the pirate.

"There are only two ships here, and they're heavily guarded," Jibs said. "Unless Darkbur's men are gonna lend us a hand, I don't see any way of stealing one."

All Shaw heard were excuses. She shot her second officer a withering look. "Well, Jibs, Darkbur's men won't exactly be aiding us in this escape, so it's time we start looking elsewhere for a ship. Plus, at least one of those is likely his."

Jibs frowned, absorbing the bad news.

Zain, meanwhile, pensively stroked his chin. "You figure Bechet's already in town, trying to help the sheriff get those meds back?"

Shaw nodded. Perhaps Bechet *was* aiding the sheriff, but only in the hopes of procuring a vessel that he and his crew could commandeer—as a reward for helping to save everyone on the planet.

It wasn't such a bad plan. Pity he'd thought of it first... if that was indeed what he was doing. The fact that he'd apparently rescued the sheriff and her people from the *Johnson* had admittedly confused Shaw. Why the hell hadn't the pirate just escaped in the med ship when he'd had the chance? That was curious. Hopefully, there was nothing wrong with the vessel itself.

"Keep a close eye on that transport you found," she said, addressing Zain. "As soon as I can get free of Darkbur and his men, we'll head to Naillik. I think we might find the med ship there isn't being guarded."

Zain's eyes narrowed. "What are you going to do, Commander? In the meantime?"

She hesitated. Should she tell them? Hell, what did she have to lose? They already knew her history. They'd understand why this had to be done.

"On the off chance Bechet is in town, I intend to kill him before we leave." She grinned. "Call it a *bon voyage* to me."

Chapter 6

REMY

"Now *this* is more like it."

While scanning the room for danger, Remy also took in the sumptuous crimson wallpaper, heavy oaken furniture, and golden lamp fixtures surrounding him. He currently stood in the ample foyer of the Butcher's Place, a hybrid hotel, brothel, and saloon. In fact, he could see the dimly lit tavern through an open doorway, and just one glimpse had assured him it was the kind of dive bar he usually favored.

Since accidentally leaving his own galaxy, this was the closest he'd gotten to the look and feel of an Earth-based residence... or, rather, one of the more popular brothels back home. The sunlight filtering through the dust motes only added to the establishment's elegant shabbiness.

"Not my style," Milo grunted. "It's the color of a mine rat's intestines."

"Don't worry," Remy assured him. "We're not hanging around for long."

If the information Dreyla and the sheriff had provided proved accurate, somewhere inside this place lay the drugs they needed to reclaim. True, it seemed a bit too obvious—not to mention ill-advised—for Gono Darkbur to conceal a planet's worth of the much-needed nano-biotics in his own base of operations. Wouldn't his competitors or any enterprising young thieves consider searching here first?

Then again, perhaps it wasn't stupidity or mere audacity that drove Darkbur's decision. Maybe it was simply the confidence of a corrupt crime lord who trusted no one would be foolish enough to steal from him. Clearly, the megalomaniac had underestimated the tenacity—and yes, foolhardiness—of the pirate from another world.

As Remy passed a gilded mirror, he did a double take. The servant's garb Lady Ris had found for him to wear was ill-fitting—the pants too short, the coat too large—but the fez managed, arguably, to pull it all together. Indeed, most people would notice the felt cap first. While Drey had remarked on its silliness, she couldn't deny that it perfectly suited the role he was playing. He would've preferred a hat with a brim, but servants apparently didn't get that luxury.

Milo approached the mirror, too. Cocking his head, he surveyed his own costume. Almost as soon as they'd arrived in Bane, Lady Ris had located a tailor and some splendid materials. Within a couple of hours, they had fabricated an authentic aristocrat's outfit. The dworg seemed positively regal.

And this was key to Remy's plan: Milo needed to appear as if he possessed some serious moolah. Initially, Remy had argued that Jacer was the obvious choice for the "rich guy" role, but that assumption was purely based on his knowledge of literary elfin societies, which apparently had little to do with real-life aflins. The dworgs, he'd been told, had a wide range of income levels, due to an imbalance of power, whereas the aflins believed in equal wealth distribution. There was just so much he didn't understand about this backwards-assed world.

As for the money itself, Lady Ris had once again stepped up to assist them. The only one with enough resources to finance their scheme, she had graciously transferred half a million credits to Milo, so he and Remy could pull off their charade.

"Let's grab a drink at the bar," Remy suggested.

What was the point of being flush if you couldn't taste the local brew? Surely, Lady Ris wouldn't mind. Besides, it was all part of the act.

He stepped aside to let Milo walk in front of him and then followed obediently, which didn't come easy for him. But he reminded himself that he'd better get the hang of it pretty damn quick, or he'd blow the whole operation before it truly began.

Since it was only midday, the place wasn't terribly crowded. At night, the miners from beyond the city limits would most likely make their way inside to spend their day's wages, while the locals would just as likely show up to ease the day's misery. But for now, the joint exuded a less rowdy vibe. Most of the patrons wore the forlorn look of unemployed hustlers and diehard alcoholics.

So far, so typical.

"I'll have one charser," Milo said in a haughty voice, then cast a dismissive look at Remy. "And give my servant here a ferrara."

The dworg seemed to be enjoying himself just a little *too* much.

The tall, lanky bartender, sporting an unruly mop

of brown, blond-streaked hair, simply nodded and stepped away to fill their order. When he returned a few moments later with their drinks, Milo handed him a card, which was imprinted with his phony credentials and contained all the credits Lady Ris had given them.

No doubt the bartender would scan the card to see how much the opulent dworg was worth. As he walked away to do just that, Milo took a sip from his cocktail. Remy, meanwhile, downed his entire glass.

"Not bad," he whispered. "Tastes just like beer." Then he belched for good measure.

Milo flashed him an annoyed look, but the bartender returned before he could reprimand his "servant."

Ignoring the dworg, Remy caught the bartender's eye.

Time to get this party started.

"My employer would also like to speak to the madam," Remy said as meekly as he could.

The bartender gazed down at Milo for confirmation and then nodded. "Yes, sir," he replied, addressing the dworg. "I will signal Madame Couche for you."

Remy laughed inwardly at the woman's name.

How appropriate.

He must've looked too amused with himself because Milo shot him a warning glance. Then the dworg's focus shifted to a point behind him.

He turned to follow Milo's gaze.

A woman approached them. Perhaps in her mid-fifties, but still quite attractive. Remy figured she'd been a working girl who'd eventually risen to the position of madam. She wore a sexy yet conservative dress with a soft woolen sweater draped across her shoulders and a pair of cat-eye glasses perched on her slender nose—the sexy librarian look.

"Madame Couche," she said in a silken voice, holding out her well-manicured hand.

Milo accepted the gesture, kissed her knuckles, and then turned to Remy, as if prompting him.

"My employer," Remy said, his gaze flitting between the madam's violet eyes and the scuffed floorboards, "would like to request the services of one of your ladies... perhaps two."

How many cons had Remy pulled in his lifetime? Too many to count.

Naturally, he'd played the role of servant before. He'd even once pretended to be a member of the high clergy on Nevis 7, and Dreyla often enjoyed reminding him of the dress he'd worn on the Prisby job. He had to admit, that one made him chuckle, too.

But this time felt different. The stakes seemed much higher.

Relax, it's just another job... no big deal.

"I'm sure we can accommodate you," Madame Couche said, a benevolent smile plastered on her face.

"Only your finest," Remy added.

The madam's ever-widening grin indicated the girls would be expensive. Very expensive. She obviously believed she had a whale on the hook.

"Please, follow me," she said.

Madame Couche led Milo and Remy to a rear elevator, which whooshed the three of them up to a suite on the twelfth floor. Soon afterward, the two men found themselves sitting stiffly on a settee made more for fashion than comfort, waiting for the madam to return with the two ladies they'd requested.

As the seconds ticked by, Remy removed his hat, fiddled with the tassel, and then donned the cap again, not sure which angle looked best. Milo, meanwhile, fidgeted with the gold buttons on his waistcoat.

The suite seemed way classier than the dive bar below—and probably most of the other rooms in the brothel. It included a spacious parlor, a kitchenette and dining nook, two luxurious bedrooms, and a pair of stylish bathrooms. Beyond the uncomfortable couch in the small vestibule, the lodgings featured a variety of plush surfaces and lavish, black-and-silver furnishings—not a speck of dust marring a single surface. Clearly, a suite intended for the wealthiest clientele.

"You know," Remy said, breaking the awkward silence, "perhaps we should speed up the plan."

Originally, he'd intended for the dworg to spend a little time with the working girls—just engaging them in conversation—while he nonchalantly explored the rest of the property. Hopefully, Milo's pretense would disarm the ladies, avoid arousing the madam's suspicion, and give Remy room to investigate any troublesome security measures.

But, really, why wait?

Milo, who'd dreaded the "entertainment" portion of the plan, quickly agreed.

"Great," Remy said. "But let's be quick. Couche could be back any minute."

From an inner pocket, he removed a vial of viscous liquid, which he'd fashioned from some hot sauce Davis had picked up in a local market and a bit of green makeup the ever-resourceful Lady Ris had supplied. Blending

45

them had created a substance remarkably similar to mocha syrup, a spot-on match for the blood of an average dworg.

Milo accepted the vial and walked toward one of the many mirrors in the suite. He dabbed a droplet on his left ear, just enough to be visible, and added another tiny amount below his right eye. The final touch: a few drops in his nostrils.

He pivoted toward Remy. "What do you think?"

In addition to the simulated blood, the dworg now sported watery eyeballs and a perspiring brow—courtesy of the hot sauce.

Remy smirked. "A vast improvement."

Milo curled his lip.

"I mean..." Remy dramatically slapped his own cheek. "Master, you look so sick."

"You know what, smart guy? You'd better go wait in there." Milo pointed to the adjacent dining area. "It would be odd if my servant allowed me to be seen with... this. Best if we pretend you hadn't noticed it at all, since it just started."

Remy considered his suggestion and then grinned. "You'd make a good pirate."

"I have no aspirations in that direction, Captain Bechet," Milo replied.

"We'll see." Remy winked at his diminutive partner

in crime.

Milo sat in the main living room while Remy walked toward a picture window in the dining nook. He had just hunkered down in an ornate but oddly comfortable chair when a knock sounded in the foyer. Remy immediately hopped to his feet and hurried to open the door, trying to maintain his "faithful servant" routine.

With a condescending nod, Madame Couche stepped inside the suite, and two Amazonian-type women followed closely on her heels. They must've been nearly twice Milo's height, and naturally, they were both stunning.

Milo stood and met them in the vestibule.

"These two ladies entertained the mayor of Yerdua when he last visited us." Madame Couche indicated the girls with a flourish of her hand. "I know dworg men occasionally prefer a woman with some height."

"Indeed," Milo assured her, craning his head to look up at them. "Indeed."

Remy shut the door and stepped dutifully behind Milo. He noticed a small drop of the fake blood threatening to drip from the dworg's earlobe.

As if on cue, one of the girls whispered nervously into the madam's ear. The woman then peered a little closer at Milo, specifically at the inflicted earlobe.

Madame Couche drew back, her thick eyelashes

batting rapidly. "I'm sorry, sir," she said in a hushed tone. "But you appear to be experiencing symptoms of the Rot. Our girls are not allowed to service anyone in an advanced stage."

Milo produced a handkerchief, wiped his nose, and stared at the fake blood with feigned chagrin. "My apologies, Madame, it seems there were some issues with the latest council shipment of nans."

"You are behind in your dose?" she asked gently.

Milo nodded. "Normally, I have reserves, but for some reason, my servant failed to keep track of them, and we ran out. I honestly suspect he may have sold them."

Four pairs of accusing eyes shifted to Remy's face. He forced a gulp.

The madam produced a tablet and scanned Milo's card. "Mr. Gimili."

Remy clenched his teeth to prevent himself from smiling. As a lifelong fan of epic fantasy, he was the one who'd come up with the slightly modified name—a reference that only Tosh had gotten.

"I think," she continued, "I may be able to help you with that."

Phase one complete.

Chapter 7

REMY

Madame Couche sniffed. "I keep telling Mr. Darkbur they need to clean this place up."

Remy followed her gaze, surveying the shabby, yellow-walled room with its crumbling plaster and cracked, brown floor tiles. Two small lamps lit the entire twenty-by-thirty-foot space, which was peppered with beaten-up chairs and couches in various states of decay.

Remy exchanged a glance with Milo. The dworg had little skill for small talk, but it wasn't Remy's place to chit-chat with the madam.

After dismissing her girls and leading the two men

from the fancy, black-and-silver suite to the ground floor of the Butcher's Place, Madame Couche had guided them through a rear exit of the bar, across a walled, bustling courtyard, and into a three-story building at the back of the sprawling property. Remy had kept his distance from the dworg and the madam, scanning each nook and cranny along the way, half-expecting Darkbur's men to spring out with guns and accuse them of various shenanigans.

Luckily, that hadn't happened, though he had noted the two meaty, armed guards standing on either side of the rear building's front entrance—and suspected Darkbur had stationed sentries behind the structure as well.

Now, he and Milo sat in a waiting room of sorts. Remy tried to act normal—though, frankly he didn't know how the servant of a wealthy, Rot-inflicted dworg should act.

Madame Couche tapped her fingernails on the desk. The young female receptionist gave a little start every time the madam paused and then resumed the lacquered drumming—seemingly the older woman's intention.

"As I said, Madame Couche, the doctor is with another client. I'm sure he'll be out soon," she said, her voice thin at the edges, and then stared at her computer screen with feigned indifference.

The madam turned toward Remy and Milo, a

haughty, contemptuous expression still emblazoned on her face. "You'll have to excuse the state of this place, Mr. Gimili. Dr. Sanger normally specializes in bod upgrades, you see. Those willing to have machines and gadgets appended to their bodies don't tend to be the discerning sort."

Remy grinned, wondering what Commander Shaw might say about that.

He glanced around the reception area, spying no signs of complex equipment or promotional materials related to the prosthetics biz. Perhaps Darkbur had shut down the body-modification shop.

"People in the market for nano-biotics are a step up from the doctor's normal clientele," Madame Couche added.

Her comment puzzled Remy. Surely body mod cost a lot, too? Commander Shaw had to have paid a mini-fortune for that impressive arm of hers or, if the rumors were true, gotten Larker Max to foot the bill.

Still, this Dr. Sanger had likely found sticking patients with syringes a simpler way to earn a living than fashioning various body parts. And with the terrible monopoly that Gono Darkbur exerted over the life-saving nano-biotics, the crime lord could demand astronomically high prices for the privilege. Much easier to exploit the desperate and the dying—and gouge them accordingly—

than to appease those seeking bionic or cosmetic enhancements.

An inner door opened, and a well-dressed woman in her late sixties stepped into the waiting room, followed by a hunched man that Remy guessed was her husband. His deeply grooved face and haggard yet strong body suggested he was a hardcore miner wrapped in an expensive suit.

"Mr. Wymer, how nice to see you again," Madame Couche said in liquid-smooth tones.

The wife shot her a nasty look.

"And this must be Mrs. Wymer," the madam continued. "Charming."

The woman tugged at her husband's arm, and his face reddened. The couple swiftly exited the building, and a discomforting silence ensued.

"Let me guess," Remy said wryly, "Mr. Wymer is a client of yours."

Madame Couche's violet eyes drilled into his face. "You are quite impertinent for a servant."

Remy almost bit off his tongue for falling out of character. He flashed a look at Milo, trying to prompt him to rectify the situation.

But Madame Couche spoke first. "Of course, you're right," she said with a smug grin. "He owns over twenty mines just north of here."

And hence is one of the few who can afford your boss's insanely priced meds.

A tablet buzzed on the receptionist's desk.

"Mr. Gimili, you can go in now," she said, addressing Milo and pointing toward the same inner door the Wymers had just used.

Remy waited for Milo to rise and step toward the adjacent room before quickly following him.

"Mr. Gimili, I hope we will see you when you are feeling better?" Madame Couche asked, her head cocked seductively.

Milo nodded and blushed at the same time. He wasn't acting, but the performance was still perfect.

Remy walked ahead and led Milo through the door into an even grungier, more cluttered space. Now, *here* was a location where he could imagine people having body mods installed.

It was a cross between a doctor's office and an electronics supplier. An examination table and assorted medical tools occupied the center of the windowless room, while fascinating, half-finished limbs of carbon alloy lay or hung everywhere along the perimeter. Wires and synthetic skin clogged up every available inch of several benches and shelves. Machines whirred and shuddered. Condensation

53

clogged the windows of various cooling chambers, making it tough for Remy to see beyond their glass fronts.

His attention turned to the doctor sitting at a large desk in the back of the room. The stocky, middle-aged man had a wide, impassive face and beady eyes hiding behind tiny round glasses. He rose to a height just a little greater than Milo's and pressed a button on his desk that remotely closed the door behind them.

"Gentlemen," Dr. Sanger said with an appraising look at Milo and a curt glance up at Remy. He tottered around the desk and shook the dworg's hand. "Madame Couche told my assistant you are in need of some nano-biotics."

"Yes, I'm afraid with the recent shipment hijacked, and my own personal stock depleted, I'm running late on my dose," Milo said, perfectly on script. He dabbed his nose with a handkerchief for emphasis.

"Please, have a seat on the examination table, and we can get this taken care of right away." Dr. Sanger gestured toward the stained, uninviting plastic mattress, the only uncluttered surface in the room. "I have to restock my inventory. I'll be right back."

While Milo complied with his instructions, the doctor disappeared through a doorway beyond his massive desk.

Remy grinned, silently thanking the universe for

the oddly perfect timing. A few seconds later, he cautiously stepped toward the half-open door and peered around the jamb, into a murky corridor. The doctor stood at the end of the hallway, swiping a key card beside a translucent door. As it opened, Remy heard the unmistakable sound of a pressurized seal giving way. A blast of frigid air rushed down the corridor, and the doctor slipped across the threshold, the door shutting behind him automatically.

Although Remy couldn't see much from his vantage point, he did observe Dr. Sanger circling a large, glowing, translucent refrigeration unit near the farthest wall of the cold-storage chamber, the door of which slid open almost immediately. He wished he could've followed the doctor—if only to examine the unit more closely—but he couldn't risk arousing suspicion or, worse, blowing his cover.

If the doctor looked up and gazed through the layers of translucent glass between them, he'd likely spy Remy's curious face peering into the shadowy hallway. So, Remy ducked back into the office and waited impatiently for his return. A few moments later, the doctor reappeared with a modest tray of vials, which he immediately slid into a small countertop fridge.

So, the storage room was unguarded—for now, at least. In addition, Remy hadn't spied any security cameras or other obvious obstacles in the corridor, but perhaps they were well concealed. More telling, though, was the fact that Dr. Sanger didn't once look back as he ventured from his office to the storage unit.

It surprised Remy that Darkbur hadn't put more protections in place for such a valuable stash, but apparently, he trusted the doctor not to run off with the goods, and the doctor, in turn, didn't seem all that paranoid about security issues during daylight hours. Perhaps he trusted the madam's abilities to vet anyone in need of his services. Having access to two beefy bodyguards—plus others throughout and around the building—likely eased his mind as well.

Good to know.

So far, Remy's plan was working. He'd discovered Darkbur's hiding place.

Of course, that was only part of the battle. Now, besides infiltrating the rear building, Remy and Dreyla would need to bust into the cold-storage chamber itself, and the fridge housing the meds was surely locked. Still, the doctor had opened it pretty damn quickly, so he'd either swiped another key card or, more likely, unlocked it biometrically, via fingerprint, face rec, or some type of DNA scan.

If he and Drey intended to succeed, Remy would have to figure out which method Dr. Sanger had utilized.

And until that point, he'd need to keep the man alive. Not that he planned on killing anyone he didn't have to. He just hoped Tosh and the gear he'd requested had made it safely through Bane's checkpoint.

Remy watched as Milo received a dose of the nans. The dworg probably needed them, so it wasn't a bad thing. The fact, however, that Darkbur's people had just charged him thirty-five thousand credits for the privilege boiled Remy's blood. The poor miners on Vox were screwed.

OK, enough.

Here he was again, thinking about something other than getting himself, Dreyla, and Tosh off this infernal planet. He couldn't forget why he'd agreed to pull off this heist in the first place.

Once Milo had thanked the doctor, Remy followed his "boss" out into the courtyard. Though he considered exploring the rest of the property—if only to avoid any surprises during the actual heist—he knew they needed to return to their hotel as soon as possible and fill in the rest of the team on the details of this crazy-ass plan.

Chapter 8

DREYLA

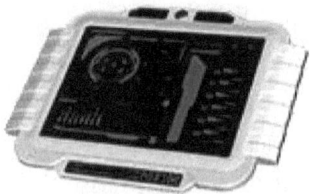

When Remy and Milo finally returned to the hotel suite where the rest of the group awaited them, Dreyla felt more relieved than she'd care to admit, especially to herself. Even better, no blood or bruises marred her father's face.

A refreshing change.

In addition, Milo, marching alongside Remy, looked none the worse for having been injected with the nans.

Dreyla had to hand it to the dworg—he was brave to

have endured the potentially hazardous ruse. If most of his race were as feisty and courageous as him, she wouldn't mind getting to know more of them. She still wasn't so sure about the aflins, though.

Scanning the group, Remy asked, "Any word on Tosh?"

Lady Ris smiled. "On his way, Captain. I will let you know when he reaches Bane."

Dreyla frowned. "Wait, he's not here yet?"

All eyes shifted toward Lady Ris, as if prompting an explanation.

The head monk grinned. "I am afraid it took us a while to track the good doctor down. Our monastery has many beautiful aspects, and it is all too easy for an inquiring soul to lose track of time."

Heads dipped as people tried to suppress their laughter. Dreyla glanced at Sheriff Lilly and spotted her lips quivering. Remy remained stony-faced, though.

"There will be two Ladies of Morbious accompanying him here for security," Lady Ris continued. "Their hovercrafts should be arriving in a couple of hours."

"Are they hiding him in a container like you did for me and the captain?" Dreyla asked.

The doc had a touch of claustrophobia, so that wouldn't go down too well.

"He suggested that he portray one of their fathers,"

Lady Ris explained.

Dreyla squirmed. The image of Tosh canoodling with the women was too fresh in her mind. Hard to envision him as a sexy monk's dad.

"Unfortunately," Lady Ris continued, "we knew that would not work, given the facial scans at the city's gates. So, yes, I am afraid he will be traveling via trunk."

Although Dreyla sympathized with Tosh's fear of tight spaces, she felt strangely relieved.

"As long as the doc has my equipment, we're all good," Remy said.

Lady Ris nodded.

"Great, then we gear up tomorrow night and get things rolling," he said.

Nobody, Dreyla noted, argued with him. Remy always considered his plans the absolute best, and at least fifty percent of the time, they worked out pretty well. Of course, the other fifty percent of his schemes often went sideways, nearly getting them all killed. But somehow, the captain would always pull himself and his principal crew out of the fire... usually at the last moment.

From Dreyla's perspective, the current plan was as solid as it could be. Since patrons often spilled out into the Butcher's Place courtyard that separated the saloon and the building housing the meds, the team could count on any decent diversion drawing attention away from the doctor's office. She and Remy had utilized the ploy of staged fights several times before, albeit usually in rowdier, more crowded situations where onlookers couldn't tell who was doing what. That part worried her a little.

Assuming the diversion in the courtyard worked, a few of them planned to glide down from the adjacent hotel and onto the roof of the rear building. There, they would breach the structure and finally work their way down to where the drugs were being kept. Then, they'd swipe the meds and get the hell out of there.

Simple.

But since none of their jobs were ever simple, Drey couldn't help but fret. While ruminating on potential catastrophes, though, she gradually sensed Remy's gaze upon her.

"Drey, what is it?" he asked, the lines around his eyes deepening with concern.

"Too simple," she said flatly.

"The plan?"

She nodded.

"Simple is good," Jacer opined. "Simple has fewer moving parts that can go wrong."

Yes, even Jacer had fallen under the captain's spell. Amazing, considering how Remy had started out on this planet as a cuffed criminal less than a week ago. But then again, this was Remy Bechet. His confidence and charm were unparalleled in their galaxy or, it would appear, in any other. He had won them all over.

Well, everyone except Lilly, whose scowls and jibes at the captain served as constant reminders that she still considered herself the leader of the pack.

"Oh, Drey," Remy said, "you worry too much."

"Someone has to," she snapped.

"The plan does seem pretty sound," Milo added, cocking an inquisitive eyebrow, inviting her to debate its merits and shortcomings.

She shrugged, unable to articulate her concern. There was still something they hadn't considered—some detail they had overlooked. She just couldn't put her finger on it.

"Relax... everyone, relax." Remy spread his arms wide. "We'll just hang low tonight. Tosh will come in with the gear. Then tomorrow night, we'll hit the doctor's office, and bam, we're outta here."

"Bam, huh?" Lilly piped up.

The sheriff and the captain eyed each other like opposing war chiefs poised for battle.

"I don't think I'll be able to relax until I'm back in my pad in Naillik," Davis said.

The others murmured in agreement.

Lady Ris wrapped her cloak around herself in a sweeping motion. "I will let you all know when my ladies arrive with your doctor."

Lilly ended her staring contest with Remy and stepped toward the head monk. "We can't thank you enough."

Lady Ris smiled beatifically. "No need to, my dear. We—everyone on this planet—are in this together."

She kissed the sheriff farewell, gently squeezed her shoulder, and then glided gracefully out of the room, followed by three of her monks. Everyone stared after the statuesque women. Everyone except the captain, who still gazed at the sheriff.

In the ensuing lull, Remy crossed the carpet between them, stopped at Lilly's side, and bent down to whisper in her ear. Dreyla tried to figure out what he was saying, but she couldn't read his lips. The sheriff, meanwhile, rolled her eyes. When he dipped his head and whispered again, she went perfectly still for a moment, a strange look crossing her face, and then offered a reluctant nod.

"Everyone, chill, we'll be back later," Remy announced.

Without another word, the two slipped into the corridor.

Dreyla gaped at the door as it closed behind them.

What the—? Ooh, men can be so stupid. Women, too.

Chapter 9

LILLY

The ground-floor saloon of the Hotel Verilux teemed with mid-evening guests. Although it might have made more sense for Milo and Remy—as the aristocrat-and-servant duo they'd portrayed—to stay at the Butcher's Place while in Bane, Lilly acknowledged it would have been far too dangerous for the rest of them. Gono Darkbur and most of his people knew their faces a bit too well. Hence, why Lady Ris had booked them a suite at the Hotel Verilux, a smaller affair than Darkbur's establishment, though no less popular with locals looking to unwind after a hard day in the city's shops and mines.

As Lilly followed Bechet through the dimly lit bar, weaving her way around patrons on chairs and stools, ignoring the curious stares directed at her, she couldn't help but chuckle. From behind, Bechet looked even sillier in his ill-fitting servant's attire. For the love of Zog, he could have taken a moment to change into his civvies, though at least he'd left that ridiculous hat back in the suite.

Her momentary lightheartedness passed, and her eyes squinted with skepticism again.

What's the wily captain up to now?

She'd only agreed to accompany him on the off chance they needed to discuss some aspect of the plan in private. It was clear he didn't want his daughter to worry about the details, and despite Lilly's mixed feelings toward Bechet, she could respect his fatherly concern.

The pirate found a table in one of the back corners. He sat in a chair and she followed suit.

Lilly crossed her arms and leaned against the table. "So, what did you want to discuss?"

He cocked his head. "Can we maybe get a drink first?"

She scowled, then nodded. He raised his hand to signal a nearby barmaid. Lilly, meanwhile, debated the wisdom of drinking alcoholic beverages with the roguish captain.

Ah, what the hell. One won't kill me.

The chirpy barmaid took their order and walked away.

Lilly drilled her gaze into the pirate's face. As Georgia, one of the monks on Trame's space station, had said, it was a ruggedly handsome visage, which had clearly borne its share of abuse—and yet had experienced plenty of joy and laughter as well. Bechet didn't possess that bitter, defeated look of some of her similarly aged deputies. She guessed he was five, maybe ten years older than she was, but that glint in his impertinent, hazel eyes told her he hadn't let the universe beat him down.

Not yet anyway.

"So, what's on your mind?" A risky question to ask such a man.

"Let's wait for the drinks."

Fine, she would sit here in awkward silence. There had been way too much talking today anyway, and far too little action.

So, she resumed her shameless perusal of him. Despite his lean frame, he was stronger and more agile than any of her deputies. Under his silly costume, he undoubtedly concealed a fit body. She'd already caught a tempting glimpse of his upper half in one of her jail cells.

He was watching her, too, his eyes darkening in the gloom of their little alcove.

After a minute, or maybe several minutes, of their renewed staring match, the barmaid returned with their order. She deftly slid their drinks in front of them and vanished into the crowd again.

While the captain had asked for a double shot of a local whiskey, Lilly had opted for a Burning Bane Special, which was currently on fire. She wondered if it was prophetic.

Bechet's lips curled into a smile. The first since they'd sat down.

"What?" she asked.

"You should put it out before the alcohol burns off."

Reluctantly, she blew into the glass, and the flame went out.

"To a successful team-up," the pirate said, raising his glass.

"No, you don't get to toast to that. This is not a team-up, Bechet. You're aiding me in a recovery effort."

"Right," he said, with what sounded like several degrees of sarcasm. His glass hovered in the air.

With deliberate slowness, she raised her drink, they clinked glasses, and their eyes met. After a few seconds, they sank back into their seats in unison.

He took a swig of his whiskey, refraining from the typical macho habit of downing the entire thing, as she sipped her cocktail. The spiciness and alcohol hit the back of her throat and drained into her chest, warming her entire body.

"Look," the captain began, his voice peculiarly strained, "I think we got off on the wrong foot."

"A strange summary of events, Bechet, given that you're a criminal. Even if you are from a different universe, which by the way I'm still having trouble believing."

"Believe it, Sheriff." He let out a long sigh. "Although, I'm not really a criminal. I'm a pirate."

"Well, pardon me for getting the terminology wrong."

The captain smiled wryly. "I do have to tread a fine line. Sometimes, my work leads me to the wrong side of the law, but I mostly deal with the outer reaches of our solar system, where the only 'lawmen' are those you've paid off and those you haven't."

She took another sip of her cocktail. His far-fetched

tale was easier to swallow with the soothing alcohol coursing down her throat and into her chest.

"Near as I can figure," he continued, "it's pretty much like living on Vox. You all seem to live by your own rules. And if the chatter in your station, and from your people, is any indication, everyone has their hand out."

"They take a little extra, that's true," she admitted. "I allow them to. They hustle to get by. We're in the middle of nowhere, and because of that, the cost of living can often be through the roof."

She pushed her half-empty glass across the table. As much as she enjoyed her cocktail, she needed to quash her thirst. She didn't like the way Bechet had her on the defensive. The pirate, meanwhile, showed no signs of stopping. He had already finished his drink and raised his hand for another.

After signaling the barmaid, Bechet turned back toward Lilly. "That's exactly the same situation we're in. I haven't been back to my planet in years." He stared down at his empty hands. "My crew and I are usually out in the farthest reaches of our system, just trying to get by." When he raised his head again, his gaze was unfocused, as if talking more to himself. "Hell, Dreyla has never even been to Earth. She's only ever seen news feeds and watched movies from my collection."

The barmaid brought him a second glass of whiskey. He hunched over the glass, still apparently lost in thought.

Then he shook his head and gazed at Lilly, his eyes sharp and bright again. "So, you see, we aren't so different."

She was about to protest his glib comparison when he abruptly redirected the conversation.

"So, what's your story? How did you come to be the sheriff in Naillik?"

"Why? Because it's hard for you to believe a woman could do such a thing?"

He lifted his hands placatingly. "I have no problem believing you're a most capable sheriff."

She hesitated for a moment, but then, whether because of the alcohol in her bloodstream or simply a sense of fair play, she decided to throw caution to the wind and divulge part of her soul as well. "My husband... was sheriff."

Bechet seemed frozen in shock.

"Yes." She nodded at his reaction. "He was killed by Darkbur's men... I just couldn't prove it... so, I took on the post." Grinning, she added, "And you can take your hands down now."

But he was looking past her, a snarl twisting his mouth.

"On second thought, Captain, why don't you keep your hands up?" a female voice rang out from behind Lilly's back.

A jolt of electricity shot up her spine. She knew that voice. Tara Shaw. Instinctively, she unsnapped the buckle on her holster and prepared to turn.

"And you can just ease your hand off that pistol, Sheriff," Shaw purred.

Lilly felt the cold metal of a weapon pressed against her back. In her peripheral vision, she noticed another one level with her face, pointing at Captain Bechet.

"Shaw," he growled.

The woman's hand tensed with the clear intention of blasting the captain's head off. The air between these two pulsed with mutual hatred. A wave of nausea crested inside Lilly's gut. This situation wouldn't end well.

"I've waited a long time for this, Bechet," Shaw said, her voice quivering with relish.

"And you'll have to wait a bit longer," another voice said. A girl's voice.

Dreyla!

Lilly could have leapt from her chair and kissed her.

Her gaze darted upward. Shaw's eyes widened, her porcelain face convulsing unnaturally.

In a flash, the captain kicked back his chair and grabbed the gun pointing at him, just as Lilly leaned to the side and yanked the blaster from Shaw's artificial hand.

Behind Shaw stood Dreyla, brandishing a small stun rod. The blonde woman continued to convulse a moment longer and then collapsed at the girl's feet.

Lilly eyed the teenager with undisguised admiration. Her own deputies couldn't have handled it better.

Dreyla prodded the toe of her boot into the body at her feet. "I suggest we get her out of here before any of her friends show up."

Chapter 10

REMY

For once, Remy felt grateful to be on the side of the law. Sheriff Greyson had capably plowed a path through the curious crowd in the murky bar, just by holding up her badge and barking "official business" at anyone who dared to step in her way. Of course, she didn't work for the Bane Police Department—no members of which Remy had yet to see—but none of the patrons in the Hotel Verilux likely knew that.

Once clear of the nosy onlookers, Remy, Dreyla, and the sheriff took an elevator up to their floor and returned to the suite they'd been using as their headquarters.

Having carried a disarmed Shaw over his shoulder all the way from downstairs, Remy was only too happy to deposit her in one of the bedrooms, her artificial arm clanking against the bedframe as she bounced atop the mattress. Dreyla and the sheriff trailed him closely, and not surprisingly, the rest of those still in the suite—Milo, Jacer, Davis, and Brand—also shuffled into the cramped bedroom to stare at the unconscious blonde woman that the four of them had only seen from afar.

Remy turned to Dreyla. "Not that I'm not grateful... but what the hell were you doing down in the bar?"

She pursed her lips. "Well, while you and Sheriff Lilly were having a cozy drink, I realized what was bugging me about our plan. The annoying little detail we'd forgotten to factor in." She gestured toward Shaw. "Since I figured she might be looking for us, I wanted to give you a heads-up. Luckily, I spotted her in the hotel foyer and followed her into the bar."

"Yeah, lucky." Remy sighed. "Wonder how she found us."

"Even with that getup..." Drey nodded toward Remy's ridiculous outfit. "...someone might've recognized you at the Butcher's Place and trailed you here. No doubt Darkbur has spies everywhere."

Two clicks interrupted their conversation. Sheriff Greyson had handcuffed Shaw's wrists to the bedframe and now lingered to examine her metallic right forearm. Based on the prosthetics Remy had seen in Dr. Sanger's office, he assumed Shaw's impressive limb was way more advanced than the usual options available on Vox. True, it wasn't as inconspicuous as those covered with synthetic flesh, but Shaw likely relished the intimidating nature of hers.

The sheriff glanced across the bed, focusing on Remy. "You care to tell me why this woman wants to kill you so badly?"

"You're looking at it," Dreyla said dryly.

The sheriff's gaze dropped to Shaw's artificial limb again, shifted to Dreyla, and finally refocused on Remy. "Whoa. You took her arm?"

"It was a work-related injury," he said.

Technically, not a lie. He'd been on a job when Shaw had threatened Dreyla, and he'd only blasted the arm off the commander's body to protect his daughter.

Sheriff Greyson's eyes narrowed. "She was the law, I'm assuming?"

He shrugged. "Of sorts. Like I told you, out in the Belt, it's pretty much the Wild West."

Her hard stare didn't waver, and he realized she probably had no clue what he was talking about.

"Look, it's as good as a free-for-all out there," he explained. "Every person out for themselves. And some even consider *themselves* the law."

"No matter who they're really working for," Dreyla added. "Anyway, her ship got sucked through the same portal as ours, and she's been gunning for us ever since."

Milo stepped beside Dreyla. "And now she's working for Darkbur?" He peered down at Shaw's lax face, sleek black outfit, and black leather boots.

"Well," Dreyla said, "she worked for an even worse pirate king back in our galaxy, so it's not surprising she's involved with a major crime lord in Bane."

The door of the suite creaked open and closed. Remy turned and spotted Lady Ris walking toward them.

He nodded in greeting, but then an awful thought crossed his mind. "Damn!"

"What?" Sheriff Greyson asked, glancing worriedly at the head monk.

Remy exhaled in frustration. "We have to pull the job tonight."

The sheriff shook her head. "I don't think—"

"Listen," he said, "I don't like it any better than you do, but if Darkbur's men can't find Commander Shaw, it's going to put everyone on high alert, which'll—"

"Make it that much more difficult to pull this job off," Dreyla finished.

Sheriff Greyson's face paled at the realization. But at least she nodded in agreement.

"Then it is excellent news that your good doctor has arrived," Lady Ris said, sweeping into the room and bestowing a smile upon each of their dismayed faces. "In fact, he has already checked himself into a suite on the sixth floor of the Butcher's Place."

Remy offered her a slight bow out of sheer gratitude. This was indeed favorable news, but even if they kickstarted the plan tonight, he couldn't leave Shaw here unguarded. He quickly scanned the room. Everyone present was already part of the plan—even Lady Ris herself. She was one of their getaway drivers, tasked with having their vehicles ready after the heist.

"Someone's gotta babysit Shaw," he said, appealing to the sheriff.

Sheriff Greyson regarded her two deputies. "Brand, you stay and guard this woman."

Both Brand and Davis opened their mouths to protest, but the sheriff held up her palm, halting them before they uttered a word.

"Since you're both part of the diversion, it just means someone else will have to pick up the slack a bit. But no matter what, Bechet's right. This woman needs to be guarded... and Brand, I think it's safe to say she's one tough bitch."

"Yeah? Well, so am I." Brand patted Davis's arm reassuringly, plopped in a chair beside the bed, and readied one of her many sizable firearms.

The sheriff nodded approvingly.

Jacer, meanwhile, had yanked off a pillowcase, rolled it up lengthwise, and pulled it around Shaw's face, stuffing part of it into her mouth. Very swift, very professional. There was more to this aflin than Remy had initially suspected. And he wasn't the only one who'd noticed. Everyone stared at the pale-skinned man as he tied a double knot with his slender fingers.

"What?" Jacer asked, straightening up.

"Nothing, that's perfect," Remy said. Then he turned back to the sheriff and clapped his hands. "Right, let's get our asses over to the Butcher's Place."

He scanned the crew. They would appear like a mob entering the hotel, and worse, half of them wore the somber expressions of folks returning from a funeral. At this rate, they would undoubtedly raise some suspicion.

He cracked a smile. "Hey, everyone, relax. Jeez, you look like someone died."

"People *are* dying, Captain," the sheriff reminded him.

"True," he said. "But we don't want to stand out. Not tonight."

Remy and Sheriff Greyson exchanged a look. For just a moment, he saw through her customary expression. He recalled how she'd appeared just a little while ago: sexy and radiant in the muted light of the bar, flushed from the alcohol warming her from within. He'd caught a glimpse of her true self, the one hiding behind the stern mask she kept so firmly in place. The story of her dead husband—it explained so much.

But right now, Remy needed to focus on the job. All that mattered was getting those meds back.

"OK, everyone, grab your gear," Remy instructed. "We don't have much time to lose."

While the team dispersed throughout the suite, and Brand kept an eye on Shaw, Remy slipped into the closest bathroom and chucked his servant's costume. It felt good to wear his own duds again.

Before leaving the bedroom that served as Shaw's temporary prison, Remy caught Brand's eye. "Seriously, this woman is no joke. Keep a close watch on her." He handed her a comms earpiece. "And let us know when she's awake." He glanced at the prostrate form of his greatest nemesis. "If she gives you any trouble, feel free to zap her again."

Brand leaned to the side and plucked the stun rod from her pile of weapons. "Will do."

Once Remy and the rest of the team were ready, he gathered them near the door of the suite. "I realize this is unexpected. Having to grab the meds tonight, I mean, instead of getting an extra day to rest and go over the plan. I know you're all exhausted. I am, too. But we can do this. Just breathe and focus on your part." He sighed, eyeing the cluster of nervous faces. "And for the love of... Spread out! I don't want everyone going in at the same time."

Before ushering the group into the hallway, he turned to Lady Ris. "So, which suite are your people and Tosh in?"

"Number 613," she replied.

"OK," Remy ordered, opening the door, "we go in carefully, in twos and threes, and then meet up at 613."

As the group shuffled into the corridor, all heads turned in perfect unison to stare at him. Like a herd of deer caught in headlights.

Oh, boy, this is gonna be so much fun.

Chapter
11

DREYLA

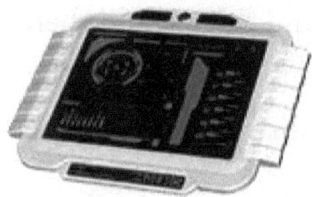

"Tosh!" Dreyla yelled.

She pushed past Remy and collapsed into the old man's chest.

Tosh enfolded her in a tight embrace.

She lingered in his arms for a moment, noting the familiar scent of his cologne—the cologne he normally used to woo women, not that the Ladies of Morbious would've required such efforts. Dreyla tried in vain to dismiss thoughts of the doctor's recent activities at the monastery. She was just relieved to see him again.

Even though he typically stayed behind on the *Jay*

whenever she and Remy embarked on a job, she didn't enjoy being separated from her two favorite crewmates (well, her *only* two crewmates nowadays) on this odd, foreign planet.

As Dreyla extricated herself and took a step backward, she noticed a ridiculously wide grin on Tosh's face. Unfortunately, she wasn't the primary cause of such glee, or at least not the only cause. Two scantily clad beauties sauntered out of an adjoining room. Actually, "scantily clad" was a stretch. Both monks had donned sheer robes—and nothing else.

Tosh gazed past Dreyla's shoulder. Wearing a sheepish grin, he joined his hands in a prayer sign. "Praise Morbious."

Dreyla whirled around in time to see Remy rolling his eyes.

The captain turned to the ladies. "Uh, yeah," he said gruffly. "We're about to have a whole bunch of guests in here."

With vague, curious smiles, they merely blinked at him.

"Um, what the captain means is..." Dreyla blurted, then searched desperately for the right words. "Well, if you could, maybe, put on some more clothes? You distract the men too much."

Heat spread across her neck, but Remy's grateful

glance was worth her momentary embarrassment. It was hard to believe she had, even for a second, flirted with the idea of joining the Ladies of Morbious. Wearing the gold-mesh bikini and flimsy burgundy robe had dissuaded her enough; prancing around naked was out of the question.

The monks smiled graciously down at her.

"We understand," one trilled.

Then, still smiling, they proceeded to a wardrobe along one wall, where they offered enticing views of their perfect bodies from behind.

Tosh watched them the whole way, a frown deepening as the women began to conceal a few of their more distracting bits.

"Tosh, focus," Remy snapped.

Once he'd snagged the doc's full attention, he filled him in on the happenings of the past day, making sure to mention whom they had lying unconscious and handcuffed back at the Hotel Verilux. Dreyla added her own commentary whenever Remy played down the good parts. She didn't, however, mention the unsettling chemistry building between the captain and the sheriff, hoping it was all in her imagination.

"Looks like I missed out on all the fun," Tosh said. He didn't look even slightly sorry.

"Oh, there'll be plenty more," Remy replied. "Come on, Drey, help me sort this gear."

She followed Remy to the two trunks in question and hunkered down to help him. Among the equipment concealed beneath the false bottoms lay several weapons—some that killed, some designed only to stun. Beyond the blades and firearms the team had already smuggled into Bane, each member would receive both a lethal gun and a short stun rod—the same type Dreyla had used to incapacitate Commander Shaw.

By the time she and Remy had organized the weapons as well as the other pertinent items, the rest of their group had arrived.

"What are those?" Milo asked.

He gazed at the short-range draft-jumpers. They resembled small sets of wings—no more than six feet wide when fully opened. A handle dangled below each wing, the grips equipped with several controls.

"We can make short-distance jumps with these," Dreyla explained.

"They're more like low-powered gliders with a very weak upper-propulsion system," Remy added, pointing at the four small thrusters under each wing.

He picked up one set of the draft-jumpers, held it aloft, and pushed a button on the handle. The wings promptly tugged at him, without lifting him off the floor.

"Luckily, they're nearly silent," he said. "But this is why we need to be higher up than our target. These will only control the descent."

"And what is this screen material?" Jacer nodded toward several rolls of black mesh lying on the floor, right next to a control line and a trigger box.

"That," Remy said with an audible note of pride, "is one of Drey's inventions."

She unfurled one to demonstrate. It spread out on the floor, covering a three-foot-by-four-foot space. "I made this from an awesome alloy back home. We hook the control line up, and it can melt through metal, ceramic, concrete, wood, or pretty much anything else, instantly creating a breaching point."

"That's clever." Lilly picked up a roll and bounced it in her hands. "Pretty light, too."

"We could use something like that," Davis chimed in. "Helluva lot easier than having to bust down doors."

Lilly nodded. "No kidding." Her brow crinkled. "I wonder, though, if Darkbur has a similar device. How else could his men have penetrated Trame's walls like they did?"

Dreyla carefully rolled up the mesh she'd unfurled. "I've been thinking the same thing."

"Well, no matter what," Remy said, "I'm grateful to have it. For breaking through Gono's roof and, if necessary, the storage unit where he's keeping the meds."

"No," Tosh warned, "you can't use it on that."

"What?" Remy pivoted toward him.

"You may damage the nano-biotics," Tosh explained. "I was tinkering with a dose back at the monastery. The nans don't react well to high heat or sudden temperature changes."

Remy clenched and unclenched his fists. "Then we'll just have to figure another way into the unit... if it's even locked."

"What's this?" Lilly had grabbed a metal cube, roughly the size of her fist.

"Easy with that, Lilly," Dreyla murmured. She gently took the device from the sheriff and turned it over in her hand. "This is another one of my inventions. It creates a plasma wall."

This statement elicited blank stares from everyone except Remy and Tosh.

"You push this button and toss it at the ground. A thin line of traxium will shoot out six feet on each side. A burst of plasma filters down the line and shoots upward, producing a wall of fire that'll seriously mess up anyone attempting to pass through it. It extends about eight feet in the air and only lasts for about ten seconds."

Dreyla enjoyed the "oohs" and "aahs" that followed, plus the general looks of approval aimed in her direction.

"Trust me," Remy added, "it's a terrific escape device. Someone's chasin' you, toss that baby down and it'll give you the extra seconds you desperately need."

"We've got some small smoke grenades, too." Dreyla pointed to the cluster of egg-shaped objects on the floor. "Good for creating cover."

Despite Dreyla's warning to the sheriff about handling potentially dangerous items, Milo crouched down and scooped up a tiny marble-sized object, one of four that Remy had just placed on the floor. Dreyla glanced at the captain, her brow furrowed in confusion.

Remy picked up another one. "Grav-speakers," he explained, gazing at Dreyla. "Wilson on Krakov 8 designed them for me. He's a fellow audiophile."

She arched an eyebrow. "And you're gonna use them for what exactly?"

"I can throw them at any surface," Remy said. "They'll stay in place for a good hour."

Her eyebrow remained raised.

"Then I blast a bit of B.B. King to confuse the natives," he added, grinning like a fool.

Dreyla rolled her eyes.

"Nice," Tosh said. "Death by music."

The rest of the group just stared blankly at Remy.

"Listen, everyone," he said, waving his hands for focus again, "if this all goes according to plan—"

"Which it hardly ever does," Dreyla interjected. She couldn't help herself.

Remy frowned, then swiftly continued. "The distraction team will cause enough of a ruckus that Drey, Jacer, and I can drop down onto the building, slip in through the roof, and nab the meds unnoticed. Ten minutes, tops."

"Ten minutes, huh?" Lilly asked, one eyebrow arched skeptically.

Remy nodded, a smug expression on his face.

"Well," Dreyla admitted, "I doubt it'll be that fast, but we intend to do our best."

Lilly sighed. "Yep, that's all we can do." She turned toward Lady Ris. "While we're busy with Darkbur's people, you and yours will be waiting in the hovercrafts. Behind the rear building."

The head monk nodded.

"Tosh," Remy said, patting the doc's shoulder. "You'll stay in the hotel and keep a lookout for us, let us know what's going on in the courtyard."

"No problem, Captain," Tosh said with a goofy grin.

"Be ready to get out of here," Remy warned, his tone sharpening, clearly trying to impress upon the doctor that he needed to focus on the mission, not the lovely ladies.

"As soon as we give the signal..." Dreyla said.

"What's the signal?" Davis asked.

"Um, when we tell you to run," Remy said, his incredulous expression indicating a silent *duh, dummy*.

"Or if it looks like stuff's gone south," Dreyla added,

"don't even wait for that."

Remy nodded in agreement.

Dreyla distributed weapons and earpiece comms to everyone in the suite, including Lady Ris and her fellow monks. After testing out the comms, the "distraction team" headed down to the saloon, where the staged argument would ensue.

Remy, meanwhile, explained the art of draft-jumping to Jacer, striving to ensure the aflin knew how to use the deceptively simple device. It pleased Dreyla that Jacer would be the one operating the wings—he seemed fairly competent.

"Tosh," Dreyla said under her breath, "the captain was serious... be ready to go."

He winked at her and puffed out his chest. "Ready as I've ever been."

His uncharacteristically macho act seemed to be meant for the monks still loitering by the wardrobe. While the rest of the team had been reviewing all the gear, the two ladies had found some colorful silk shawls to drape over their luscious curves. If anything, the women looked even more alluring now.

"Well, that just fills me with confidence," Dreyla muttered.

Chapter 12

SHAW

Shaw cautiously opened her eyes, letting in a chink of light. Her heart raced, and thoughts dribbled into her mind, laboriously and painfully, but she knew enough not to make any noise. What had hit her? A stunning device. Was she otherwise hurt? No. The pain clustered in her head, back, and wrists.

Her pulse calmed down a notch. The last thing she remembered was staring down at Bechet, pointing her gun at him. Once again, the pesky pirate had managed to escape. But who the hell had knocked her out from behind?

Based on her limited perspective, she lay on her side atop a mattress in an unfamiliar hotel room. Likely in the Hotel Verilux, somewhere above the bar she'd last encountered Bechet. She tried to shift her arms, but they seemed to be secured to the thick metal bedframe. With a careful tilt of her head, she surveyed her wrists and recognized the type of handcuffs she'd seen in the sheriff's office. OK, this confirmed her theory that Bechet was still working with the law.

Or pretending to.

A young, blonde woman sat in a chair beside the bed, gazing out a nearby window with an unawareness that indicated boredom and a tragic lack of experience. Shaw had seen her before... somewhere. Yes, she was one of Greyson's deputies, though she didn't appear to be in uniform. She, Bechet, the sheriff, and their irritating cohorts were all probably trying to blend in with the locals.

A stinging pain radiated out from the small of Shaw's back, but she forced herself to focus on her right wrist. The artificial sensors weren't identical to flesh-and-bone receptors, but they simulated familiar sensations, adequately informing her the cuff was loose enough for what she wanted to do. If she pulled her hand downward, she could flex it open while twisting at the wrist, which might, in turn, break the cuff. Whoever had secured her hadn't factored in the extra strength of her artificial hand. How foolish of them.

Bechet should know better.

"No, she's still out," the deputy said, flicking her gaze to the bed.

Shaw quickly shut her eyes and feigned unconsciousness. The comms unit, presumably a hidden earpiece, would make her escape tougher.

"Yes, I'm sure," the deputy continued in a piqued tone. "Her breathing hasn't changed."

Who was she talking to? The sheriff? Where was Bechet in all of this? And why hadn't he thought to knock her out with a heavy-duty sedative? He had to have suspected the stun rod wouldn't provide a lasting effect. Maybe the deputy was supposed to electrify her again if she awakened too soon.

Shaw risked another peek beneath her barely open eyelids. The woman stood up, stretched, and, with a leisurely pace, walked out of her line of sight. Her footsteps changed from padding on a soft, absorbent surface to clicking on something much harder. Apparently, she had moved into a different room, probably a bathroom, given the hollow sounds of the woman's shoes.

This was the moment. Shaw tugged her right hand downward, flinching as the pain receptors scraped against the metal cuff. Biting down on the soggy gag in her mouth, she opened her palm and twisted her wrist hard.

A satisfying snap told her the cuff had broken. As she freed her artificial arm, the other cuff still clapped onto her left wrist clanked against the bedframe.

Damn.

The deputy appeared, open-mouthed, in the doorway of the bathroom. She made a move toward her hip to draw her pistol, but Shaw was too fast. She sprang to her feet, broke the other cuff with her powerful right hand, grabbed the chair beside the bed, and whipped it across the room. It struck the deputy in the torso, making her stumble backwards.

In a flash, Shaw darted across the bedroom, pushed the stunned deputy to the floor, and pinned her arms with her knees. Two deft strikes to the temples, and the deputy's head lolled to the side, her eyes closed. Still alive, but in for a rough awakening. Her pretty little face wouldn't be so pretty for a while.

Shaw untied the cloth around her head, rose to her feet, and scanned the room properly. The pungent, sweet scent of aflin hung in the air. She'd first noticed that distinctive aroma upon meeting one of Darkbur's Elocin contacts. She also caught the smell of ladies' perfume, plus human sweat. Perhaps Bechet's.

Her gaze drifted through the doorway, noting the rest of the suite. No doubt there had been others here recently. Wherever the sheriff's people had gone, their plan must already be well underway—a plan, no doubt, to reclaim the stolen meds. What else would've lured them to Bane?

Did she care? Not really.

Should she care? Also, not really. She had no loyalty to Darkbur. Why should she risk her neck getting involved in something between him and the law? Especially since the crime boss didn't seem to employ anybody truly faithful to him, much less anyone who actually liked or respected him. Darius certainly didn't.

She would let this situation play out as an objective observer, waiting for an opportunity to strike. If whatever the sheriff and Bechet were doing could possibly help her get off this dump of a planet and back to her own solar system, she would be ready. And if the chance to shoot the pirate arose again, she'd be double-ready. This time, she wouldn't let the moment slip from her grasp.

After scooping up her weapons, which some moron had conveniently dumped in a corner of the room, she leaned over the unconscious body of the hapless deputy, removed her comms earpiece and her pistol, and then swiped a large rifle leaning against the wall.

This girl must love her guns.

After kicking the rest of the deputy's weapons beneath the bed, Shaw crept through the silent suite and into the empty corridor.

Time to check out what's going on. I have a feeling things are about to get interesting.

Chapter 13

REMY

"And there he goes," Jacer said, tapping his earpiece.

Over the comms, Remy heard the beginning strains of the argument meant to kick off their diversion. Down in the seedy bar, Milo bellowed at Davis over some fictitious offense, something about an unpaid round of drinks. That dworg sure had a powerful set of pipes. When Remy, Dreyla, and Jacer glided over the courtyard, they'd be able to witness the performance firsthand.

For now, though, the three of them (plus Tosh) had to enjoy it from afar as they padded down the hallways and up the stairwells of the L-shaped Butcher's Place, striving for speed but often having to slow to a dawdling pace whenever they encountered any hotel or brothel guests. An exhausting endeavor, but they couldn't afford to raise suspicion, especially given the folded wings and other paraphernalia they carried.

Remy wished that, upon Tosh's arrival in Bane, he could've secured a suite facing the rear courtyard, but even sporting a disguise, the old doc hadn't wanted to press his luck. Fortunately, though, one of the Ladies of Morbious had managed to lure another hotel client out of her twelfth-floor suite, which just happened to overlook the courtyard and the rear building.

As the phony argument raged downstairs, Remy and his three companions hastened through the side wing of the Butcher's Place and finally arrived at the appropriated suite.

"Stay back," Remy cautioned as he shouldered open the unlocked door. "Lemme make sure the coast is clear."

After verifying the suite was indeed vacant, Remy ushered his three cohorts inside, secured the door, and made a beeline for the bedroom offering the best view of the courtyard. He turned down the lamplight and motioned for the other three to remain out of sight while he stepped toward a large picture window and studied the scene below.

Night had fallen, which would help to conceal their descent, and mounted floodlights illuminated the courtyard, enabling Remy to survey the situation. A pair of guards still flanked the front door of the rear building, but a small crowd had formed on the opposite side of the courtyard, near the open doorway of the saloon.

After a moment, Remy gestured to Dreyla and Jacer, indicating it was safe to join him at the window.

"As soon as our guys draw the guards' attention, we jump," Remy told them, pointing toward the two armed men far down below. He turned to the doctor. "Tosh, remember, you just stay here and keep a lookout for us. You'll be our eyes once we breach the building."

"You got it, Captain."

Hoping Tosh would remain focused, Remy opened the window as wide as possible, secured his draft-jumper, and crouched on the windowsill. He jerked his head around to see how Dreyla and Jacer were holding up.

"You two ready?"

Dreyla had accomplished far more hazardous jumps than this, so she didn't seem nervous in the least. She just smiled back gamely, arranged her satchel full of gear, and spread her wings.

Jacer, however, was busy playing with the control grips of the draft-jumper, steadfastly refusing to look at either him or Dreyla. Remy had been around the aflin long enough to know that he was insufferably proud, so attempting to reassure him would likely backfire.

"It'll be fine," Remy said.

The aflin stopped fiddling with the handles and glanced at Remy. "Yes, I am sure your daughter will be fine, Captain Bechet." His voice sounded wobblier than usual.

A loud slam resounded below, followed by even louder yelling. Milo and Davis had done the first part of their job to perfection, their fight spilling across the threshold of the saloon. Remy watched as the two guards stormed across the courtyard toward the point of disturbance. The rest of the crowd homed in on the ruckus near the doorway, their excited voices echoing off the structures and walls that enclosed the courtyard.

"Now," Remy ordered.

He leapt off the windowsill and, once clear of the building, fired his thrusters. The wings caught the air, yanking him forward and downward at once. He rather enjoyed using the draft-jumpers, which mimicked the sensation of real flight. Not like a spaceship or an old-school airplane, but rather like a bird. So visceral. Not only could he feel the air rushing upward to greet him, but the thrusters actually fired in a bird-like flapping sequence.

Dreyla sailed past him, flashing him a huge grin.

The kid relished this as much as he did. Though he appreciated seeing her in such a good mood, he wished it didn't have to happen under these life-and-death circumstances.

Remy had almost forgotten about Jacer. He adjusted his glide path and glanced around him. Where the hell was the aflin? He craned his neck to look back at the open window.

Oh, crap.

Jacer hadn't budged from the windowsill.

"Come on, man," Tosh said via their linked earpieces. *"You gotta do it. Just jump."*

Remy couldn't yell at the aflin, afraid to alert the guards in the courtyard, so he offered a vigorous nod instead, hoping Jacer's pale eyes could see him in the near darkness. But the aflin remained frozen in a crouch, silhouetted by the low lamplight behind him. For all Remy knew, the aflin thought he was saying it was OK to stay behind.

Dammit.

Ahead of him, Dreyla had almost reached their target. With utter ease, she had descended the nine flights from the hotel's twelfth floor to the top of the three-story building at the rear of the courtyard. She landed gracefully, softly touching down on the rooftop, and collapsed the jumper.

Remy was only seconds behind her. He hit the building a little harder, mostly because the Jacer dilemma had distracted him. The aflin had finally stepped off the windowsill. The only problem now: He hadn't activated the thrusters right away and had consequently plummeted over five stories before engaging them.

At least he was still high enough that nobody on the ground had noticed him. Remy held his breath, expecting Jacer to yelp after the initial drop. To the aflin's credit, he didn't utter a sound.

Dreyla stepped beside Remy. "He looks scared."

"Petrified."

Together, they watched in helpless silence as Jacer headed toward them, jerking downward like a pelican with a broken wing caught in a hurricane.

"But, you have to admit, he is pretty funny-looking," Remy said, mainly to conceal his own nervousness.

Vaguely illumined by the lights in the courtyard and the surrounding hotel rooms, Jacer continued to descend at a haphazard pace. His long hair flew behind him, and his mouth had fallen agape, fixed in a silent scream.

"He reminds me of a famous painting," he added.

Dreyla nudged him with her hip. "You're a sick man, Captain."

"I know." His grin faltered. "Crap."

Judging by his cockeyed angle, it looked as though Jacer was going to miss the roof altogether. Remy bounded toward the edge of the building, praying the aflin wouldn't land in the courtyard and foul up the entire scheme.

Jacer cut the power to his draft-jumper just as he reached the edge of the rooftop, but as predicted, his feet slipped and his body tilted backward, aiming for the ground below. Remy reached outward, caught the aflin by his belt, and yanked him onto the roof, but the momentum made Remy lose his balance. He staggered backward, tripped on his own feet, and landed hard on his ass, Jacer flopping across his outstretched legs.

Remy winced. "Oomph."

Dreyla sauntered up to them and gazed downward with a mischievous glint in her brown eyes. "Fun, wasn't it, Jacer?"

The aflin rolled off Remy's legs and remained kneeling on the ground, steadying himself. Eyes wide and shell-shocked, he still managed a supercilious retort. "No, it certainly was not. But that was not the purpose of the exercise, was it, Dreyla?"

She and Remy glanced at each other, biting their lower lips to stifle their laughter.

While Drey extended a hand to help the aflin to his feet, Remy stood up and stepped toward the front of the building. Carefully, he peered down into the courtyard. Nobody seemed to have noticed their antics in the air, thanks to the commotion that Milo and Davis had created. Unfortunately, though, the crowd was already starting to lose interest and disperse.

Remy, Dreyla, and Jacer didn't have much time. They had a roof to rip open.

Chapter 14

LILLY

"Sorry about this," Milo whispered to Davis, just loud enough for Lilly to hear via the comms.

Davis gazed down at the dworg, a blank expression on his young face. Before he could protest, Milo grabbed his arms and flung him into the center of the crowded courtyard. Lilly winced as her deputy slammed against the concrete, landing on his left shoulder. The dworg sure possessed more strength than his short stature would indicate—not unlike the rest of his stalwart species—and he had a terrific flair for the theatrical.

"I warned you, boy!" Milo yelled, wiping away some spittle with the back of his sleeve.

Davis slowly rose to his feet, shaking his fist at Milo, and stumbled around in a daze. Lilly worried about his stability, but a sideways glance reassured her: He obviously wasn't as dizzy as he pretended, and his sense of humor was fortunately still intact.

"And I'm sorry about this, my friend," Lilly whispered, summoning all her strength.

She lifted her boot and kicked Milo in the lower back, sending him flailing towards Davis. The two armed guards, who had rushed across the courtyard toward the ruckus, burst through the curious onlookers and split apart, just in time for Milo and Davis to stumble between them. Startled, the guards both crashed into some hapless onlookers on either side of the crowd. Lilly's gaze shifted back to her compatriots, who had fallen beside one of the two centrally located fountains.

Perfect choreography, you two.

Lilly glanced around the courtyard. A handful of patrons from the Butcher's Place had been standing outside at the start of the argument. Now, several more clustered around the scene, wearing expressions of renewed interest since angry words had evolved into actual fighting. Although she felt grateful for the successful diversion, she wished that some of the nosy patrons would wander back into the saloon and out of harm's way.

With a smidgen of reluctance, she drew her pistol. Two of the loitering patrons winced and edged toward the rear building.

Milo, meanwhile, had rolled to his feet and grabbed Davis's back. He pretended to use the deputy as a human shield while brandishing his own weapon. Lilly had to swallow her laughter. It was rather comical, after all, watching the short, stocky dworg pushing the much taller man in front of him.

"Not gonna shoot your boyfriend," Milo hollered.

Lilly unleashed a fake-hysterical guffaw—one she'd learned from Yercer Taul. "Go ahead. Then I kill you. Even trade."

She raised her gun. Milo moved to one side, still gripping Davis with one hand. She carefully let off a shot behind him, near enough to make it seem as though she'd just missed. The shot hit a gutter near the roof of the rear building. With a minor explosion of rusted metal, the downspout toppled away from the structure and crashed beside a woman standing at the far end of the courtyard, spraying brownish sludge all over her.

Damn, that's gonna hurt.

The buildup in Bane's gutters could be highly acidic, burning through clothes and skin alike. Lilly made a mental note to visit the woman later and have the Naillik Police Department cover her medical expenses.

"What the hell are you people doing?" the tall brunette cried.

Instead of darting toward the saloon and tending to her acid-soaked clothes, she started screaming. The sludge must have penetrated her outfit.

A hefty man, probably her boyfriend or husband, tried to tear the offending shirt off her, which only made her scream louder and beat his chest with her fists. Lilly wrenched her gaze away from the side drama to check on their own situation. If this wasn't a diversion to beat all diversions, then what was?

The two guards had disappeared into the jostling crowd, but Lilly was smart enough to keep a lookout for them—and any of Darkbur's other hired minions.

Milo, meanwhile, continued to hold Davis captive and hide behind his human shield. Davis played along nicely, both hands up, a look of sheer terror on his face.

"You piece of crap," Lilly yelled. "You lost that hand fair and square!"

"Like hell, girly! When your boy here wasn't stiffin'

me for drinks, he was doin' nothing but cheatin'," Milo retorted. "Has been the whole night!"

Lilly heard a commotion behind her. Half-turning, she noted a new group of bar patrons in the doorway, all of whom jostled for a better view of the ruckus in the courtyard. No doubt the blood-curdling screams of the acid-soaked woman had convinced them it was a brawl worth watching. They advanced slowly in a tight pack as more and more curious patrons pushed forward from inside the saloon.

Contrary to all her instincts, Lilly whirled around and aimed her pistol at the newcomers. A moment of stunned silence ensued, a collective intake of breath followed, and then all at once, the crowd scattered, people shrieking and ducking in all directions. The courtyard filled with the sounds of terror and chaos. Lilly couldn't have orchestrated a more satisfying result.

The two guards reappeared, spinning around in confusion, pointing their guns every which way. Clearly, they didn't know what to make of the situation.

Which was exactly the point.

Chapter 15

REMY

As the sheriff and her two cohorts upped the stakes down below, Remy paced off five steps from the front corner of the roof and then knelt to unfurl Dreyla's mesh. He and Milo, as the aristocrat-and-servant duo, hadn't been able to scope out the upper floors of the building during their fake emergency visit to Dr. Sanger, but they had luckily noted a set of stairs beside the doctor's office. With a little luck, Remy, Dreyla, and Jacer would drop into the stairwell, unseen by any lurking guards.

Dreyla sank to her knees and busied herself hooking up the controller box to the mesh. A year ago, Remy had asked her to conjure up some easier way of breaching a spaceship, particularly when connected via the *Jay*'s umbilical. He'd intended the project to keep her mind occupied as they traveled through the long, boring stretches of the cosmos, and if it worked on space-worthy vessels, Remy had also considered using it for other structures, such as space stations and asteroid-based buildings.

Well, Drey had outdone herself. This mesh could win awards. Secure patents. Remy even envisioned the potential ads on the broad-wave: *Need to bust into a bank? How about breach your neighbor's house?*

Undoubtedly, the stuff could even disintegrate the sturdy walls surrounding the monastery in Trame—which, like the sheriff, had made him wonder if Darkbur possessed a similar tool.

The design brief he'd prepared for her was simple: He wanted a controlled cutting tool that could penetrate the hull of any targeted vessel, no matter the material, without causing a lethal depressurization and killing everyone in the umbilical as well as the opposing spaceship. After all, why should people have to die for the sake of stolen goods?

Larker Max had called the innovation pure folly, preferring his crews to blast open their quarry's ships, venture inside wearing enviro suits, and grab whatever they were supposed to steal, no matter who perished along the way. Larker had never appreciated the subtle notion of life preservation. One of many reasons Remy had despised working for him.

For this job, reclaiming Vox's med shipment, Remy had considered using Drey's invention to breach the rear wall of the building—instead of relying on their aerial stunt—but depending on how long it took them to bust into the refrigeration unit and nab the meds, he'd worried about passing guards or pedestrians noticing the giant hole in the wall before they were ready for a firefight.

"I've never actually used this version," Dreyla said, her face taut with anxiety.

"Sure you did," Remy replied. "That time in Sector 9 on—"

"That was just a small opening. This here's gonna disintegrate the entire section."

Remy shot her a look. "Something wrong with it?"

"No..." Dreyla's eyes darted to each corner of the mesh. "I'm just freaking out, I guess."

Remy patted her shoulder. "Hey, you've done at least ten scarier things than this since we fell through that portal. Now's not the time to doubt yourself."

"But this is..." Dreyla swiped away several sweaty strands of her curly hair. "I mean, have I scaled it up correctly? Have I gotten the math right?"

"Yes. Yes, you have," he reassured her. "Now let's

bust into this joint."

His attention switched to Jacer, who crept toward the front of the building, probably to snag a glimpse of the cacophonous diversion currently underway. Lilly and Milo were staging a Shakespearean performance down there, complete with plasma blasts, enraged shouts, and an ever-loudening chorus. Remy wouldn't have minded getting a look himself, but he didn't want to risk being seen or catching a stray shot.

"Stay back, Jacer," he cautioned. "They might see you... and then the jig's up!"

Jacer froze mid-stride and stepped back from the edge. After a brief hesitation, he joined Remy in watching Dreyla trigger the device. With a final loud exhale, she pressed the button. The mesh lit up prettily—a glowing, sizzling, electric-blue square of pure destruction. A few seconds later, a section of the concrete ceiling had vanished along with the mesh. Nothing remained but a spacious, precisely cut opening and the lingering smell of various burnt aggregates.

Single use, but damn useful. Almost as elegant as magic.

Remy glanced at Dreyla and arched an eyebrow.

She smiled back grimly and hastened to pack up the triggering device.

He gazed down into the hole. As the smoke cleared, he realized that, just as he'd hoped, they would drop directly into the stairwell.

"We need to hurry," he whispered, gathering his gear.

He was poised to lower himself into the building when a shadow appeared in the third-floor doorway. An armed man had entered the stairwell but apparently hadn't noticed the hole in the ceiling yet. Easier to miss on a moonless night.

Don't look up. Please don't look up.

Remy's frame went rigid. Feeling quite exposed with his legs dangling below the ceiling, he tried to remain perfectly still as he waited out the man below. But when the guard refused to budge, Remy twisted his torso to face Dreyla and Jacer, who crouched nervously behind him, and pressed his forefinger to his lips.

With the infinite skill of a longtime pirate, he quietly secured his equipment bag, holstered his pistol, and unsheathed a stun rod. Then, he leaned over the opening, gripped the edge of the ceiling with one hand, slipped into the hole, and rocked his body forward. Before the guard spotted him, he catapulted himself into the hapless minion, slammed him against the doorjamb, and, after scrambling to his feet, zapped him with the stun rod.

Between the hard whack to the man's back and the shocking voltage that followed, the guard predictably collapsed. His motionless body slid down a few steps, his head thudding against each one—but he didn't descend far enough.

After relieving him of his weapons and comms device, Remy had to drag his heavy body to a corner of the third-floor landing, so Jacer and Dreyla could lower themselves into the building.

Once the three of them were safely inside, Remy motioned to them for silence, tried to ignore the courtyard din coming through his earpiece, and listened for any nearby footsteps, particularly the thuds of backup guards running to the scene of the breach. Nope, nothing but the usual hum of air-conditioning units.

"Hey," Tosh's voice sounded through Remy's comms, startling him. *"Where are you guys? The courtyard's pretty bright, but I'm having trouble making out the other building. Even with the binoculars."*

"We're alright, Tosh," Remy whispered. "We're inside the building. Just keep a lookout for us, but try not to talk unless you have to."

"OK, Captain."

"Should we take out any guards on this level?" Jacer pointed to the third-floor doorway.

Remy shook his head. "No time for that." He gestured toward the stairs. "Come on, let's do this."

Although he'd feel more relaxed pulling a heist in a building devoid of any active guards, he always preferred evading confrontation if possible. With a little more luck, they'd grab the meds and escape the building undetected.

Or rather...

He stepped gingerly over the stunned guard's outstretched arm.

...without further detection.

Chapter 16

LILLY

"Brand?"

Lilly winced, trying but failing to conceal her horror as Deputy Brand pushed through the wall of patrons still lingering at the threshold of the Butcher's Place and stumbled into the courtyard.

Blood dripped from gashes near her temples, and bruises marred her normally pretty face. She swayed a little, probably exhausted from the effort of hurrying from the Hotel Verilux in her condition, and she seemed to be missing her usual arsenal of firearms. Not to mention her comms earpiece.

Although Lilly had had her doubts about leaving such a newbie to guard Tara Shaw, she hadn't had much of a choice. She'd needed Davis for the distraction, and everyone else had a necessary job. She wished she could've brought more deputies on the journey from Naillik to Trame, but she knew the Ladies of Morbious could only smuggle a small group into Bane.

Ah, well, we work with what we have.

Lilly hoped a liberated Shaw wouldn't complicate matters, but for now, she was grateful—if perplexed—that the mysterious woman had left her deputy alive. Messed up, but alive.

"Sorry, Sheriff," Brand panted. "She got away." Then, as if realizing her mistake, she clapped her hand over her mouth.

Craaappp.

The two armed guards in the courtyard were too dimwitted to comprehend Brand's words—or at least connect the dots—but the brawny man bolting to attention in the doorway had certainly grasped the deeper meaning. Lilly recognized the muscular tank of a man as another of

Gono's pet goons.

"Tell Mr. Darkbur we got Sheriff Greyson," he yelled to someone inside the saloon.

Lilly grabbed Brand and tugged her behind one of the fountains in the center of the courtyard. The weary deputy sank to the ground in a semiconscious state as Lilly considered her options.

Milo, clearly grasping that Brand had inadvertently blown apart their plan, released his clutch on Davis and aimed his pistol at one of the two guards. Davis drew his own weapon and targeted the other one. The problem? Both guards were aiming back.

For a moment, nobody fired. Lilly's mind whirled, attempting to sift through all the variables. She couldn't tell the difference between the criminals and the innocent bystanders, so she really didn't want to start shooting anybody.

Many patrons were still caught up in the situation. While some had scattered and bolted at the sight of Lilly's gun, others had simply taken their place. Some had even brought their drinks outside while they watched the melee. Why the hell didn't they take cover inside? Were they that stupid, or were they so accustomed to nighttime showdowns that they considered this one just another form of free entertainment? No doubt if any of her people died in the ensuing firefight, the onlookers would consider it a bonus.

The beefy minion in the doorway brandished his weapon, and three more of Darkbur's goons shoved their way through the crowd, guns held aloft.

Still, nobody fired. Milo and Davis maneuvered to the other side of the courtyard, behind the second fountain, but the porcana statue at its center was much smaller than the broncan one mounted on hers—and wouldn't provide one stocky dworg and one sizable human male much cover. It would have made more sense for her and Brand to crouch behind the smaller fountain, but it was too late to switch places now.

"Sheriff Greyson," Gono Darkbur's voice rang out, his tone one of feigned politeness. "I'm assuming you're trying to break into my building?"

Lilly's gaze shifted toward the open doorway of the saloon, where the crowd parted reverentially to let the crime lord pass into the courtyard.

She peered around the broncan statue. "Only recovering what you stole, Gono. Give yourself up now, or it's only going to get worse for you."

Darkbur chuckled. "There's no way you're getting out of this courtyard alive."

"Then I might as well take my shot," Lilly muttered. She stood to her full height and leaned around the statue, just enough to get a good aim at the man.

Unfortunately, the hefty brute was too fast. Just as Lilly squeezed off a round, he yanked a young man from the crowd and ducked behind him so that her plasma blast hit the hapless spectator square in the chest.

Oh, no!

"Kill them," Darkbur yelled. "Kill them all!"

Then he flung the young man to the side, plunged through the crowd, and vanished into the saloon. The man Lilly had accidentally shot sank, lifeless, to the ground.

Lilly's stomach roiled, but she had no time for regret. Her own life was on the line.

More of Darkbur's goons stomped through the doorway. Luckily, the dispersing crowd hampered their progress. Apparently, seeing the dead man crumpled on the concrete finally woke up the rest of the onlookers. Now in full panic mode, people tossed away their drinks and tried to flee the courtyard, clambering and clawing their way past the goons, back into the saloon.

Amid the chaos of screams and broken glass, both sides of the battle opened fire.

Blasts collided with the buildings, the benches, the statues, and the few remaining saloon patrons unlucky enough not to have scrambled out in time. Lilly cringed at the pointless carnage.

Clenching her jaw, she crouched beside the fountain and managed to take a clean shot at one of Darkbur's men—the big guy who'd outed her. The blast hit him in the shoulder and knocked him to the ground.

She pivoted to focus on another guard near the saloon, and a blast whizzed past her face so close she felt the hot air whip her cheek. She whirled to the side. The man she'd just shot wasn't dead—or even unconscious. From his position on the ground, he had propped himself on his elbows and aimed his rifle at her head.

As she retreated, he took another shot, which blasted into the edge of the fountain's pool. Water gushed out into the center of the courtyard, drenching Lilly's boots.

She knelt behind the broncan statue for cover, trying to keep an eye on the scene but unsure what to do next. Davis and Milo knelt behind the smaller porcana statue, shooting toward the growing group of men filtering into the courtyard, all aiming to kill them—painfully, if possible. Milo ceased firing long enough to pluck one of Bechet's smoke grenades from his satchel. After arming it, he tossed it toward the men.

Immediately, the area filled with a thick, dark-green smoke. It hadn't reached Lilly yet, but she took a bracing breath of slightly fresher air in anticipation.

Oddly, though, the smoke stayed put, suspended in a billowing shape, almost as if it were a solid entity.

How bizarre.

Captain Bechet and his daughter had certainly brought an impressive box of magic tricks with them.

With all of Darkbur's men trapped inside the greenish cloud, the shooting soon tapered off, and a much-needed moment of relief ensued. When one of the goons stepped through the green cloud and into the open air, he left a man-shaped opening behind in the smoke.

Lilly gaped at it, momentarily forgetting her job. Luckily, Davis reacted more quickly, hitting the man directly in the face with a plasma blast that hollowed out his head and left his torso a gratuitously bloody mess.

"That's disgusting," Milo said.

"Crap." Davis peered at the barrel of his rifle.

Lilly frowned. "You had it on full power?"

"Yep, and now it's drained." Sighing, Davis threw down the rifle and drew out his pistol.

Milo's face crinkled in confusion.

"Set at full power, I only had a few shots," Davis explained. "Takes ten minutes to recharge."

"Well, this ain't lasting ten minutes," Lilly grumbled.

Nobody else had emerged from the smoke yet, but it was only a matter of time.

Davis glanced at Brand, who, after resting for a few moments, had finally opened her eyes and risen to her feet. No doubt the cool water, which had drenched her pants as it flowed from the busted fountain, had done its part to rejuvenate her.

Davis's brow furrowed as he noted the full extent of her facial injuries. "Are you OK?"

Brand fiercely shook out her limp blonde hair. "I'm good, I'm good."

She plucked a small blaster from her ankle holster, which Shaw had apparently missed during her escape, and clicked off the safety catch. Ignoring Davis's concerned looks, she stood alongside Lilly and aimed her weapon at the dense cloud of green smoke.

"Bring it on," she growled with a determined menace Lilly had never before heard from her deputy.

Chapter 17

DREYLA

"What the hell?!" Remy yelled, just as a red plasma bolt streaked mere inches from his scruffy face.

Quickly and quietly, Dreyla had followed him and Jacer down the staircase, through an empty reception area, and into the oddest-looking doctor's office she'd ever seen. Fortunately, they hadn't encountered any more of Darkbur's guards along the way, but from Remy's tone, she figured their unusual boon of good luck had just run out.

Dreyla peered down the dimly lit corridor that ran behind the office—or, rather, the chamber resembling a mad scientist's lab. At the end of the hallway stood a translucent door, through which she spied the refrigeration unit where Darkbur had apparently stored the pilfered meds. A narrow walkway encircled the large, squarish unit, which glowed with a strange blue light, and its only access door lay on the other side, near the farthest wall of the room.

How could she tell? Because the same translucent material that composed the door blocking their path also made up the upper half of the cold-storage enclosure. Probably this world's version of transparent steel.

As fascinating as all that was, she had other things to focus on. Like whatever had just tried to shoot her father—and, thanks to proximity, *her*.

After breaching the rear door of the office, the two of them had immediately stepped into the secret hallway— and almost immediately met a barrage of plasma blasts.

Ducking to avoid another deadly streak of red light, she noticed some movement at the end of the shadowy corridor. "Captain, did you see that?"

Remy stepped in front of her, shielding her from any additional blasts, and followed his daughter's gaze.

"Holy crap," he muttered. "We're in a bit of trouble. Back up... NOW!"

On instinct, she peeked around him. Her eyes had finally adjusted to the murkiness, enabling her to see what had uncharacteristically freaked out the captain. A dozen robotic, spider-like drones scurried along the floor, the walls, even the ceiling, and naturally, each appeared to be heavily armed. And exceedingly pissed off.

Remy whirled around and, with paternal urgency, shoved her toward the open door of the office. She stumbled backward and across the threshold.

"Ergh," the captain yelped as he darted into the room, just two steps behind her.

One of the blasts had obviously connected with his flesh. As Dreyla leaned against the wall beside him, attempting to stabilize her breathing, she spotted a singed mark on his right shoulder.

"You're hurt," she said. An unnecessary observation.

But in typical Remy fashion, he ignored the wound and focused on the problem at hand. "Course it couldn't be easy," he grumbled. "When is it ever?"

She grimaced. "Pretty much never."

"OK, gimme a minute to think. There's gotta be a way past them."

Hard to fathom how Remy could concentrate with all the chatter on their comms. Drey wanted to remove the earpiece, but unfortunately, they had to stay linked with the rest of the team—just in case the sheriff required some assistance.

Hell, at this rate, we might need some help, too.

In the meantime, she just wished the others could fight less noisily.

"What is going on?" Jacer whispered, bringing her back to their present dilemma.

Though they'd left the armed aflin to stand guard near the doorway between the reception area and the office, he'd since taken several steps toward them.

"Guess we tripped a trap of some kind," Dreyla explained, her heart pounding in her chest. "Never seen that before..."

"Never seen what before?" Jacer insisted.

She met his concerned gaze. "Robotic spiders. Armed robotic spiders."

"The good doctor probably activated them before leaving for the day," Remy mused. "An ingenious, if inconvenient, security system."

"Didn't you see them earlier?" Jacer asked. "When you and Milo cased the joint?"

Remy frowned. "Clearly not. Otherwise, I would've let Dreyla know *before* entering the hallway." He turned toward the open door—and the eerily quiet corridor beyond. "I don't think they'll come down here unless we try leaving this room again. They're obviously meant to keep intruders from reaching the cold-storage area."

Testing his theory, Dreyla stepped past him and poked her head around the doorjamb.

A split second later, a strong hand grasped the back of her jacket and yanked her downward. Luckily, the captain's timing was impeccable. As she dropped to the floor, several plasma blasts penetrated the doorframe, precisely where her face had just been.

Wincing, she glanced at Remy. "Sorry."

"That was dumb, kid," he snapped, his brow furrowed. "Don't do that again."

"Heavens." Jacer retreated a few steps. "You two were not kidding."

Dreyla and Remy scrambled to their feet and resumed their stance against the inner wall. Embarrassed by her near-fatal mistake, Drey said nothing. She merely watched her father, who stared straight ahead, a stony expression on his face. One hand still gripped his stun rod—which would surely be useless against armed spider-bots—while the other gently stroked his beard.

Drey knew that gesture well. Meant Remy was in strategizing mode, which typically led to an insane plan that might get them all killed.

She smiled, despite the desperate situation. So far, none of his half-baked ideas had resulted in their untimely demise. No matter how dire the circumstances, her father had always managed to pull them through alive. Well, at least where he, she, and Tosh were concerned.

Remy had certainly lost his share of loyal subordinates over the years. Like poor Newman. Just the latest in a long series of deceased crewmates. An inevitable occurrence in their line of work: Since smuggling jobs and other acts of piracy were illegal, most were incredibly dangerous, too.

While waiting to hear the details of Remy's latest scheme, Drey abruptly recalled one of their craziest jobs ever. The one involving the *Cosmic Reality*, a humongous starship that ferried tourists around Earth's solar system in top-of-the-line luxury. With the staff included, the vessel held roughly four thousand people and featured every possible amenity, from fancy shops and spas to swanky bars and restaurants, plus a multiscreen movie theater and a high-stakes casino. Remy had told her the *Reality* reminded him of the cruise ships that sailed Earth's oceans.

Impressive, if you like that sort of thing. Which I typically don't.

Along with all her other amenities, the starship naturally contained several banks. Where else would all those uber-rich people safely store their money? Didn't they require easy access to their funds while playing high-risk card games, purchasing overpriced outfits, and springing for decadent meals? But, of course, they did. And unsurprisingly, Remy had had the grand idea of robbing one. Not an easy task in the remote blackness of space, but when had that ever stopped the daring pirate?

At the time, Dreyla had doubted the success of her father's scheme—especially since, to get him and his chosen crewmates on board, Remy had decided to play the ol' ship-in-need-of-aid trick. Not an unbelievable ploy, considering the *Johnson*'s rough exterior. Though an amazing, tried-and-true ship, she didn't look particularly spaceworthy from the outside. Still, while the *Jay*'s weathered condition and doctored credentials might fool the powers-that-be, the crew likely wouldn't. Whoever ventured onto the *Reality* needed to resemble employees aboard a lawful cargo ship—not a bunch of rough-and-ready pirates.

To sell his cry-for-help story, Remy had chosen his youngest crewmates to accompany him—guys with fewer battle scars and even fewer bad habits. Though not part of the captain's initial selection, Drey had pleaded so relentlessly that Remy, who usually couldn't stand to disappoint her, had ultimately allowed her to join the team.

At the very least, he figured, the presence of an adolescent girl might minimize any suspicion cast on him and the other ruffians.

In the end, five crew members boarded the *Reality*: Remy, Gurgan, Drey, Thomas, and Terry. According to the captain, the plan was simple: pretend to be stranded cargo-haulers, smuggle some guns aboard the luxury star-ship, locate and rob one of the banks, and make a speedy getaway.

Meanwhile, back on the *Johnson*, the remaining crew members would miraculously "fix" the supposed engine problem. So, by the time the five pirates had plundered the loot and returned to the ship, the *Jay* and her crew could promptly disappear into the black.

Predictably, though, the job did not unfold as intended. To sell their ruse, Remy had ordered his fellow pirates to dress in their finest (or, rather, least-weathered) attire and stagger the timing of their off-ship excursions. Gurgan, a reliable young man who'd lived on the *Jay* for over a year, ventured onto the starship first, shortly followed by Thomas and Terry, two handsome brothers who'd only been part of the *Jay*'s crew for a few months.

Remy had dubbed them "the Terrible T's"—not because they were vicious and violent (cuz they weren't) but because they were awful pirates. Neither of them could shoot particularly well or think quickly on his feet, and thanks to a nasty gambling habit, they'd often find themselves in sticky jams, impossible to escape without the captain's help.

But whenever Drey wondered why Remy kept them

around, she'd remember that they were loyal, hardworking, and eager to please her father. Didn't hurt that they were also handy mechanics, not to mention attractive, confident, and charismatic enough to serve as worthy distractions for a bank job. In other words, they would act as both eye candy and lookouts while Gurgan, Remy, and Dreyla snuck into the bank via an air-conditioning duct, incapacitated a few guards and employees, and breached the vault.

No doubt Remy had hoped the gig would offer the two brothers some much-needed pirating experience, but sadly, they only ended up embodying their nickname. While they'd played the role of cargo-ship crewmen convincingly enough to enter the bank without provoking suspicion, all it took for them to slip out of character was a tempting posse of hot rich chicks who stopped to flirt with them.

Although the five pirates had separate tasks, they were all linked via comms. So, while gathering as much currency as they could carry, Drey, Remy, and Gurgan heard the two idiots go off script and brag about their pirating prowess. Remy instructed the fools to stop blabbing, but the order came too late. A passing security guard had already heard and confronted the braggarts, and a gunfight rapidly ensued.

Cursing under his breath, Remy sent Gurgan toward the lobby to help the Terrible T's out, but as soon as the young man stepped outside the vault, a plasma blast hit him directly in the chest. Although Remy managed to wound the security guard who'd killed Gurgan and relieve him of his weapon, Dreyla and her father both knew it was time to bolt.

Originally, Remy had intended to grab the goods, seal all the employees and customers inside the bank, and jam their external comms, allowing him and his cohorts plenty of time to make their escape. But once the skirmish broke out and the plan went sideways, Remy's main priority was getting Drey back to the *Jay* as safely as possible.

So, after securing their equipment satchels and money-filled backpacks, the two of them unleashed a couple smoke cartridges, which enabled them to flee the vault, dart through the bank lobby, and reach the shopping concourse. Thanks to the roaring battle and blaring shipwide alarms, however, they couldn't sneak back to the *Jay* unnoticed—which was especially true once additional reinforcements arrived and managed to gun down the Terrible T's. The entire security force would now focus their energies on finding and killing Drey and Remy.

Without looking back at their fallen shipmates, the two of them sprinted down a serpentine ramp and across a spacious atrium filled with actual plants, trees, and, yes, even grass. Drey might've considered the bustling chamber quite picturesque had they not been running for their lives.

As well-dressed pedestrians ran for cover, Dreyla trailed Remy through the foliage and behind an unassuming maintenance shed, where they could momentarily rest and figure out their next move. Luckily, they were crouching less than a hundred yards from the corridor leading to the loading dock where they'd parked the *Jay*. Not so luckily, they could see a slew of security officials searching for them, and they knew that, in no time at all, the powers-that-be would realize the crew of the *Jay* had caused the disruption. At that point, a clean getaway would be utterly impossible.

Drey had been about twelve years old then and, though skilled with computers, not accustomed to firefights or madcap lams. So, she'd simply stayed hidden and let her father do the thinking.

Now, four years later, Remy wore the same pensive expression he'd sported back on the *Reality*. As he leaned against the wall, just around the corner from the murderous spider-bots, he continued hatching a defensive plan that would undoubtedly seem just as bizarre and improbable as most of his other ideas. That was simply how he operated. Equally risky and resourceful, he'd conjure up a far-fetched, harebrained scheme that sounded utterly ridiculous and yet somehow succeeded.

Well, sort of.

Usually, the only variable he couldn't predict was the behavior of other humans—which often proved to be a pretty critical factor. If the Terrible T's, for instance, had followed his instructions on the *Reality*, they and poor Gurgan probably wouldn't have died in an unnecessary gunfight. And he and Drey wouldn't have ended up in such a dire predicament.

Dreyla sighed wistfully at the memory, then impulsively grinned as she reflected on the rest of their misadventure.

Four years ago, while she and her father crouched behind that stupid shed, she had quietly watched as Remy gazed into the distance, stroking his beard and trying to fathom a way out. Abruptly, he spied two trash receptacles—one on either side of a nearby tree. Sporting stiff, rectangular shells painted in gold filigree, they were indeed the prettiest garbage cans Drey had ever seen.

After ensuring the coast was clear, Remy jogged toward the tree, plucked the fancy covers off the two cans, and returned to their hiding spot. Before Dreyla could question the move, he handed her one of the covers and told her to slip it over her head. As she stood there, contemplating how her father had finally lost his mind, he merely grinned, lowered himself toward the grass, and pulled the ornate frame over his entire body, laden backpack included.

With just his head visible through the solitary opening, he explained the plan: The two of them would mosey toward the loading dock camouflaged as garbage cans, and if anyone crossed their path, they would simply duck down and keep still until the person wandered away.

"Saw it in a movie once," Remy told her. "They might think they're going crazy for a second, but eventually, they'll move on."

She remembered telling him it was easily the stupidest suggestion she'd ever heard from anyone. In response, he'd simply nudged her with his stinky disguise until she finally unleashed a dramatic sigh and tugged her own cover over her petite frame. The darn thing might've made a garbage can seem less unsightly in the gorgeous atrium, but it sure didn't smell as pleasant as it looked. It was also rather uncomfortable, especially with the heavy money satchel hanging from her back and one of the equipment bags strapped across her chest.

She opened her mouth to protest, but Remy cut her off with another nudge, his garbage-can disguise bumping into hers.

"Let's go."

Following a quick scan of their surroundings—momentarily free of people—the two of them rose to their feet and headed through the atrium, toward the passageway that led to the loading dock. Even while advancing toward their destination, they kept a lookout for potential witnesses. Hard to believe they were alone, but it seemed the battle in the bank had temporarily scared off any curious passersby.

Dreyla silently thanked the universe for their solitude. One, because she didn't fancy getting nabbed by the authorities, and two, because she and her father looked utterly ridiculous.

Of course, their good luck didn't last. About a hundred feet down the passageway, she heard distant voices and footfalls.

"Duck!" Remy instructed in a stage whisper.

Immediately, she crouched toward the floor and shimmied backward, abutting the nearest wall. Remy did the same right beside her.

Peering through the gap where people usually deposited their trash, Dreyla observed a pair of armed security guards bolting down the passageway. Carefully, she drew the small plasma blaster she'd smuggled on board the *Reality*. If the guards had observed their absurd stunt and were headed their way, she wouldn't get pinched without a fight. Remy was undoubtedly thinking the same thing.

Luckily, the guards darted right past them. Once they'd vanished from sight, a hollow chuckle emerged from the other trash bin. Clearly, Remy was impressed with himself. His foolhardy garbage-can disguise had worked.

After ten minutes of stops and starts, they managed to reach the loading dock without incident. Through the large transparent force field that filled part of the far wall, Drey spied the outer dock where they'd left the *Jay*. Fortunately, she was still there, ready and waiting for her missing crew members.

Despite the shipwide alerts urging passengers to beware of two escaped fugitives, the dock workers didn't seem fazed. They just bustled around as usual, unloading crates, sorting supplies, and repairing machinery. And oddly enough, no security guards had yet arrived.

So, before anyone spotted the out-of-place trash-can covers, Remy and Drey ditched their smelly disguises and made a beeline for the umbilical linking their ship to the *Reality*. Just as they reached it, however, a security team bolted onto the scene, shouted for the workers to clear out, and promptly opened fire.

"Knew our luck was too good to last," Remy grumbled as he pushed Drey into the umbilical and whirled around to defend himself.

Drey figured the powers-that-be had traced their path via hidden security cameras—or finally realized it was no coincidence that a mysterious cargo ship had arrived just prior to a bloody bank heist. Either way, it was time to go.

With a few well-aimed shots, Remy managed to keep the guards at bay long enough for Drey to enter the *Jay* and mobilize the remaining crewmates. Then the captain shut the umbilical door, jammed the lock, and retreated to his ship. Before the furious guards had a chance to follow him, Remy retracted the umbilical, released the docking clamps, and got the hell out of there.

Yes, Drey and her father had escaped that time, but the captain had always regretted losing his men.

Men, ha. They were just boys.

Witnessing the deaths of Gurgan and the Terrible T's had haunted Remy for a long time. That little cruise-ship mishap had also urged him to be even more protective of his daughter—which both comforted and irritated Drey.

Back in the present, Remy snapped his fingers, suddenly ending her reverie.

"The *Reality*," he murmured.

Dreyla grinned.

Like father, like daughter.

Remy tossed the stun rod atop his satchel and scurried toward the closest filing cabinet—a sturdy structure, hopefully made of a plasma-resistant metal alloy. As Drey and Jacer watched, he cleared it of all miscellaneous debris, yanked out all the drawers, sawed off the inner supports with the serrated knife he usually kept on his belt, and painstakingly crafted four ragged holes in the rear panel: two small ones for his eyes and two larger ones for his hands. Then he ducked his head, squished himself inside, and teetered around to face them.

A tight fit, but he seemed to have enough room to draw his Colt and aim it through one of the holes.

Dreyla giggled. "You look ridiculous."

From the bemused expression on Jacer's face, she knew he shared her opinion.

But as usual, Remy didn't care about his appearance. He just winked at her through one of the eyeholes. "Wait here." Then he shuffled toward the doorway and slipped into the corridor.

Immediately, red-hot plasma blasts streaked past the room, and a medley of gunshots, clanks, and manly grunts assaulted her ears. After half a dozen shots from her father's Colt and several more from his plasma blaster, she heard a yelp, followed by a loud metallic thud.

Almost as willful as her father, Dreyla raised her blaster and edged toward the doorway. She didn't fancy getting shot, but she couldn't abandon her captain either.

"He said to wait here," Jacer reminded her.

With a wink of her own, she sprinted into the hallway. Ducking to avoid an errant blast, she spotted Remy dodging two separate volleys. The filing cabinet lay in a crumpled heap against the back wall, several dents and gashes evident, and the remains of ten disabled spider-bots lay strewn across the floor.

Unbelievably, Remy had managed to destroy most of them before having to abandon his compromised "armor." But the two currently targeting him were still a problem. Only took one well-aimed shot to do the job. Especially if he was low on ammo.

Crouching toward the ground, Drey pointed her blaster at one of the remaining spider-bots and opened fire. In a flash, it pivoted away from Remy and trained its plasma blasts on her.

While she bobbed, weaved, and kept up her own assault, Remy shot her a concerned gaze, tossed his weapons to the ground, and zipped around the security drone still focused on him. Maybe he didn't want to damage the cold-storage area with a wayward blast. Maybe he was out of ammo. Maybe seeing her in trouble had motivated him to end the standoff.

Whatever the case, Remy grasped two of the spider-bot's articulated legs and, as the others wriggled and slashed at him, repeatedly slammed the critter against the wall. In less than a minute, the spider-bot had shattered amid a shower of sparks and flying debris.

As for the final spider-bot, Drey had managed to shoot off two of its eight legs, but despite its lopsided movements, it still had a fully functioning defense system. In fact, several deadly blasts forced her to dive behind the disabled cabinet for cover. The spider-bot responded by scurrying awkwardly up the wall, likely to get a better shooting angle. Peering over the cabinet, Drey was unable to get a bead on the speedy thing.

Luckily, though, the captain was done being polite. He whipped out his giant knife and hurled it through the air, ultimately pinning the bot to the wall. Then he grabbed one of its dismembered legs and bashed its head until it caught fire and fizzled out.

"See?" He grinned, turning toward her. "No problem."

Rising to her feet, Dreyla couldn't help but return the grin.

He squinted. "But next time I tell you to wait..."

"Yeah, yeah, yeah." She strutted toward the cold-storage area. "Let's just get the meds."

"Hang on a second. Gotta reload."

Reluctantly, she followed him back to the office, where he'd left his gear.

Jacer met them in the doorway. "Everything alright?"

"For now," Remy replied, grabbing his satchel. "Just keep an eye on the front. We've got more work to do."

Chapter 18

REMY

Remy drummed his fingers against his holster. "Can you get it open?"

He and Dreyla stood on the narrow pathway between the wall of the cold-storage chamber and the translucent door of the well-secured, walk-in refrigeration unit. Overriding the key-card device in the corridor had been a cinch for his whiz kid. But the unit housing the meds posed a greater challenge.

Initially, Drey had planned to use her wonder device to burn a sizable hole in the appliance—large enough for them to crawl inside and grab the meds. But thanks to

Tosh's experiments in Trame, she suspected the intense heat might ultimately damage the delicate nans. She'd also told Remy that she worried about tripping a pressure detector, which would, in turn, set off a deadly booby trap. Something worse than armed spider-bots. A poisonous gas maybe.

Deep in concentration as she inspected the complex lock, she didn't pause to answer Remy's question. Perhaps she hadn't even heard him. Despite her intelligence and resourcefulness, she no doubt found it difficult to focus on her task with all the yelling, shooting, and general mayhem coming through her earpiece comms. Remy had temporarily removed his as soon as they entered the storage room, just so he could hear himself think.

Figuring Jacer, who still stood guard in the doctor's office, was linked to the rest of the group, he almost suggested Drey remove hers, too, when he noticed the bruises on her young face. His chest tightened with anger. His stomach knotted with guilt. And he once again thought about tracking down the brute who'd struck his daughter in that filthy alley—just as he had when she'd first returned from her recon mission with a bloody nose.

Ultimately, though, it was all Remy's fault. He was the one to blame for every injury she'd sustained and every danger she'd faced over the past eight years—ever since he'd rescued her from the slavers on Kofax Prime and welcomed her aboard the *R.L. Johnson.*

Though only eight years old at the time, she'd proven to be a tough, capable child, and while he'd initially treated her as little more than an adopted daughter, it hadn't taken long for her to embrace the uncertain life of a space pirate, with all the adventure, hard work, and perils such an existence entailed.

Sometimes, he regretted what he'd allowed to happen. Not saving her from the asteroid mines—he'd never second-guess that. But even though he'd grown accustomed to her presence on the *Jay*'s bridge—and heavily relied on her mechanical and navigational skills—he knew he'd never forgive himself if Dreyla ever suffered a serious wound or, worse, succumbed to death on his watch. And he certainly wouldn't let the perpetrators go unpunished. Hell, even those who'd merely threatened her safety had paid a steep price: Tara Shaw had lost an arm, and Urgon Joss had forfeited his entire life.

Trying to shake free of his guilt-ridden thoughts, Remy shifted his gaze to the glassy door of the cooler, through which he spied several metal shelves filled with vials and boxes of all shapes and sizes. Naturally, he only cared about the two dozen crates lining the lower shelves, which matched Sheriff Greyson's description of the stolen nano-biotics, but unfortunately, they lay just out of reach.

Remy needed Dreyla to focus her considerable engineering skills on busting the door wide open.

From what he could tell, the lock wasn't linked to a DNA scanner of any kind. Good news, considering they had no idea whose DNA they'd have needed—whether Dr. Sanger's, Gono Darkbur's, or someone else's altogether. But as he'd suspected, the system did involve biometrics of some kind: specifically, a peculiar handprint screen, unlike any he'd ever seen before.

"So? Can you do it?"

Dreyla looked up at him and shook her head, her bouncy brown curls belying her grim expression. "Maybe if I had half an hour."

"We don't have that kind of time." He sighed. "Can't we just blast through it?"

"No. The door's reinforced. And anyway, you might destroy the meds."

Crap. Only one option left.

"OK, wait here." Remy set his bag on the ground. "That damn doctor must be in the building somewhere," he grumbled, racing toward the door they'd propped open. "At least he'd better be."

He bounded down the hallway, zigzagging through a minefield of spider-bot debris. As he burst into Dr.

Sanger's office, Jacer sprang to attention, his weapon thrust far too close to Remy's face for comfort.

"Just me, Jacer," Remy said, easing the tip of the gun to the side. "Stay here with Drey, will ya? I'll be back in a flash."

The aflin nodded and resumed his post.

Remy winked at him, grabbed the blaster he'd left leaning against the wall, and slung its strap over his shoulder. Although he'd already reloaded his trusty Colt, he figured a second gun might come in handy if he encountered any armed guards in the building—a distinct possibility, given his loud-ass battle with the spider-bots. Besides, someone might've discovered the zapped goon in the stairwell. For all he knew, a platoon of Darkbur's minions were headed this way.

Leaving the door to the corridor open so Jacer could keep an eye (or at least an ear) on Dreyla, Remy wove his way through Dr. Sanger's disorderly office and technology lab. As before, he noted all the artificial appendages stuffed on the shelves, including arms, legs, eyes, and other obvious body parts. This time, though, a large phallic device snagged his attention, and while every second counted, he couldn't help but pause to check it out.

Whoa. Why would anyone want a mechanical one?

True, horrific accidents could happen, even down there, but still...

With great effort, Remy attempted to erase the image from his brain as he cautiously crossed the adjacent reception area. Surprisingly, despite the maelstrom raging outside, no one had yet invaded the building via the front door facing the courtyard. The sheriff and her distraction team were obviously holding off Darkbur's thugs.

As soon as Remy entered the stairwell, he removed the earpiece from his pocket and reactivated it. Immediately, his ears filled with shouts and gunfire.

"Sheriff, how's it going out there?"

"Actually," she said via the comms, *"we're kind of pinned down."*

His stomach clenched at the sound of her strained tone.

"Just—just hold on," he said desperately. "The storage unit has an unusual lock, but we're working on it."

"Hurry, Remy," the sheriff pleaded. *"We can't hold out much longer."*

It was the first time she'd ever willingly used his first name, a fact that made him feel equally comforted and alarmed.

Not sure how to respond, he dashed up the stairs instead. A plasma blast hit the wall only inches from his face. He glanced upward and spotted an armed guard leaning over the railing on the third-floor landing. Just as the man pulled the trigger of his blaster again, Remy ducked sideways, raised his own gun, and sent a bullet straight into the assailant's exposed neck. With a startled cry, the man fell forward, his bulky torso yanking him over the railing, and plummeted past Remy as he reached the second-floor landing.

"We're gonna need to get you in here," Remy finally said over the comms.

"No way," the sheriff protested. *"There's no exit out of that building."*

"I know. We'll make our own."

He dashed into the second-floor hallway and glanced around frantically. Good news: No other armed guards had yet gotten wind of his presence. Bad news: At least a half-dozen doors lined the corridor, any of which could possibly conceal the doctor. But which one was he hiding behind, and was he even on this floor? Or, hell, still in the damn building?

"Hold them off just a couple more minutes," Remy said. "We'll get those meds, I swear."

Remy held up his pistol and kicked in the first door. An empty bedroom greeted him. Whether it was used for medical recovery or as an extension of the main brothel, he didn't know—and didn't care.

"Hurry!" the sheriff's voice implored amid a crackle of gunfire. *"We don't have a couple minutes!"*

"Roger that," he said as a plasma blast came through the wall on his left, the one facing the courtyard, and penetrated the opposite wall. "Crap!"

Motivated by the desire to avoid an accidental headshot, Remy kicked in the second and third doors. Two more vacant bedrooms.

Just then, he heard a squeak—from a woman or perhaps a child. Somewhere nearby. After busting through the fourth door, he felt an uncanny jolt—a helpful sixth sense—and ducked to the side just as a plasma streak flew past the young receptionist he'd met on his earlier visit. Her naked frame was twisted awkwardly toward the door, but even in the dim lighting—and despite the distracting blast that had hit the wall behind him—Remy could see she was straddling the doctor he sought.

"I don't want to hurt you," Remy said, holstering his Colt and raising the plasma blaster.

As he set the deadly piece to the lowest power setting, another shot hit the doorjamb, forcing Remy to hide behind the wall. After a few tense seconds, he peered around the doorframe again.

"Get out or you're dead!" Dr. Sanger shouted, his tousled head appearing from behind the receptionist.

The hand holding his blaster shook so much, the

man had zero chance of hitting a moving human target. He'd only gotten lucky with the doorframe.

But just in case Remy had underestimated the doctor's shooting skills, he retracted his head, pointed his blaster around the doorjamb, and squeezed the trigger three times. Then he quickly advanced into the room, only to find the doctor and the receptionist cowering on the disheveled bed. Both winced at him, gingerly fingering the fresh scratches and burn marks on their faces and bodies.

The lowest setting might singe exposed flesh, but the effect was the equivalent of getting hit with a hundred-mile-an-hour gust in a hot, sandy desert.

They'd both live. *If* they cooperated.

Remy kicked away the blaster the doctor still clutched. The stunned receptionist, meanwhile, blinked once and then, as feisty and enraged as she was slim and sexy, promptly slapped Remy on the cheek.

He grasped her fingers before she could withdraw them and squeezed tightly. "Honey, you can do so much better than this guy."

His gaze flicked to the naked doctor, still blubbering empty threats. He'd half-expected to spy a wondrous phallic enhancement between his legs.

Nope. All organic and definitely not wondrous. More like miniscule.

She could certainly do better.

Moving his gaze upward, Remy noticed the doctor's other hand. In fascinated horror, he released the receptionist.

OK, so there is a gizmo involved in this scenario.

Instead of an artificial hand, the doctor had attached a phallic device to his right wrist. The same size as the contraption Remy had just spotted down in the lab, maybe even a bit bigger.

During his initial visit with Milo, he hadn't even noticed the doctor's artificial hand. As his eyes shifted to the nightstand beside the bed, he realized why. The default appendage lay next to the lamp, its realistic fake-flesh coating impressive even in the murky light. Even better, he could discern the unusually striated fingerprints, the ones matching the strange locking mechanism on the refrigeration unit.

Without hesitation, and despite the doctor's protests, he snatched up the hand, grabbed the gun on the floor, and bolted through the doorway.

"Bechet, we're in trouble!" the sheriff's voice rang out via his earpiece comms.

"Drop all the grenades," he ordered with frenzied

glee, holding tight to the pilfered pistol and the bizarre hand-shaped key. "Drop 'em all now, Sheriff! And head for the rear building!"

Already halfway down the stairs, he wanted to be ready to greet the rest of their party and finish this fiasco once and for all.

Chapter 19

LILLY

Lilly peered around the base of the broncan-topped fountain, wondering if Bechet's advice was solid. Even if his handy grenades provided decent cover, could she, Milo, and her two deputies really make it to the rear building without catching an inconvenient plasma blast in the back?

Gono Darkbur appeared in the doorway of the Butcher's Place saloon. "Throw down your weapons and we—"

Even before Lilly could raise her gun in protest, a

plasma blast obliterated his words. Missing the infuriating crime lord by mere inches, the shot had come from Milo, who still crouched next to Davis behind the smaller fountain in the courtyard.

"Ugh," the dworg grunted.

The weirdly dense cloud of green smoke produced from one of Dreyla's odd inventions had cleared enough for Lilly to see the enemy—and to recognize that Darkbur's numbers had increased. At least a dozen armed men had joined the fight, dispersed on either side of the crime lord along the edge of the courtyard.

"He asked for it," Lilly shouted. "Everyone, drop your smokes. All of them. Now!"

She activated and tossed hers into the middle of the brightly lit courtyard, between the two fountains. Milo threw one towards the open doorway of the saloon. And Davis rolled his closer to the rear building. She expected more of the forest-green smoke, but instead, puffs of gold and purple particles exploded from the grenades, intermingling like vivid paint in a bucket of water.

Dreyla definitely had a sense of humor.

The entire courtyard filled with thickening clouds of solidified dust. Darkbur's men couldn't see the small cluster of interlopers through the kaleidoscopic haze, but unfortunately, Lilly and her crew couldn't see anything either, not even one another.

"Run for the rear building!" she ordered Davis and Milo via the comms.

Brand remained beside her, standing in a stiff, trancelike shooting position, her gun pointed forward, as if tracing Darkbur's movements through the colorful fog.

"Come on," Lilly urged, tugging her deputy's arm. "We'll get him another time."

As Lilly fumbled her way through the dense smoke toward the rear building, white-hot plasma blasts flew on either side of her, puncturing the strangely stationary haze. Most came from the enemy behind her, but based on the direction of the shots, someone on her side was obviously shooting back to keep Darkbur's men at bay.

"Be careful, you fools," she hissed as one plasma blast sailed only inches past her. "You might hit one of us."

Eventually, her boot scuffed the wall of the rear building. At least, she hoped she'd reached her target. Hard to tell when you couldn't see more than a few centimeters in front of your nose.

Someone collided with her backside. She whirled around and spotted Davis, who had reversed toward the rear building with his gun pointed forward. No doubt he'd been the one shooting back at Darkbur's goons.

A few seconds later, Milo joined them.

"Brand?" Lilly asked the two men.

No answer. From them—or from Brand, who had

lost her earpiece during her unfortunate tussle with Tara Shaw.

"Brand?" Lilly repeated, wishing she'd dragged her deputy from the fountain instead of trusting her to follow.

Dammit, where is she? What's wrong now?

Behind her, she heard a lock disengage, followed by the sound of someone flinging open a door. Hopefully, it was the front entrance of the rear building. She prayed, too, that Bechet was the one standing on the other side of that unseen doorway, or she and her cohorts might well be screwed.

With a smidgen of hesitation, she crept along the outer wall of the building, toward the open door. Milo and Davis slipped ahead of her as she fired her blaster toward the saloon, hoping to prevent Darkbur's gunmen from narrowing the distance between them—and silently pleading that she didn't hit Brand in the process.

As Lilly and her companions reached the doorway, Bechet's head appeared around the doorjamb. Before she could stop herself, an unabashed grin spread across her sweaty face. She'd never been so happy to see that scoundrel's mug.

Bechet guided Milo into the building, quickly followed by Davis. But Lilly lingered outside, still worried about her newest deputy.

"Sheriff, get your ass in here," the pirate shouted.

"Brand?!" Lilly cried once more, facing the wall of vibrant smoke behind her.

Bechet gripped her left shoulder and tried to pull her backwards, but she resisted fiercely.

"No, let me go," she cried as she wrenched herself free.

Several blasts hit the outer wall of the building, on both sides of the open doorway. Lilly returned fire in the shooters' direction. A loud yelp of agony rang out. She'd hit one of Darkbur's men.

The pirate grasped one of her arms again, this time with a stronger, viselike grip, and swung her inside with such force she lost her balance. Toppling forward, she braced herself for a hard, painful impact and landed instead on something slightly more pliable: Remy Bechet.

He'd apparently fallen on his back in a dimly illumined reception area, and she lay sprawled ungracefully on top of him, her left hand splayed across his chest, her right hand pressing against the scuffed tiles beside his chiseled jaw, still clutching her blaster.

Behind her, the door slammed shut, and a barrage of blasts pummeled its outer surface. Some penetrated the door itself while others seemed to rock the entire building. Milo and Davis darted past her, into an adjacent room.

Lilly shuddered, and Bechet's hand tightened around her right hip.

She tore her gaze away from Bechet's darkening eyes and gingerly peeled his hand off her body. "Brand's still out there," she growled, rolling off him and leaping to her feet.

She marched toward the door, ignoring the gunfire aimed in her direction, grappling for a plan to rescue her stubborn deputy.

"Uh, we gotta move," Bechet said, grasping her hand and tugging her across the room.

She wanted to resist, but another stray blast convinced her otherwise. Once Bechet managed to pull her into the inner room and slam that door shut as well, she swung around to face him. Something about him seemed off.

Well, more off than usual.

Besides his holstered Colt, he had a pistol tucked behind his waistband and a blaster hanging from his right arm. Her gaze traveled downward, and her vision doubled. Bechet had two right hands. No, wait—he was holding a *severed hand!*

"What the hell's that?" she shrieked.

Bechet grinned and turned the artificial palm upward, revealing a set of strange fingerprints. "Our key to the safe."

She blinked, but before she could think of a response, he turned and bolted toward Jacer—and yet another open doorway.

"Guard that door," Bechet called, flapping the prosthetic hand at the flimsy barrier between the reception area and what resembled a mad scientist's workshop.

The pirate dashed past the stony-faced aflin and into the rear corridor.

Milo sidled up to her. "What the hell was that?"

"Must need it to get into the nano storage," Lilly mused.

She turned to secure the door behind her and spotted Davis pacing frantically across her path. Guessing the reason for his agitation, she approached him cautiously.

"Where's Brand?" he demanded.

Lilly cocked her head toward the door.

Davis's eyes filled with terror. "She's... still out there? But—"

"Maybe she headed for another way inside," Milo suggested.

"I'm not sure there *is* another way inside," Lilly lamented.

Davis flung open the door and bounded into the reception area, but at the same moment, another volley of blasts pelted the front entrance. He ducked instinctively, clenching his fists.

"If that damn room had a window," Milo growled, peering around the doorframe and scanning the hole-peppered front wall, "we could hold them off a bit longer." Sighing, he retreated toward Lilly. "But as it stands, our best bet is to stay in here."

No more than a minute or two would likely pass before Darkbur ordered his men to storm the building. The only thing delaying them was their complete lack of vision inside the hazy courtyard, but that hadn't made them any less dangerous. Just more haphazard.

"Dammit, Davis," Lilly hissed. "I'm worried about her, too, but we can't look for her now. We need to guard this door and give Bechet and Dreyla the time they need to free the meds."

Davis glanced back at her, his eyes radiating worry, anger, and frustration. Though Lilly shared his emotions, she steadfastly refused to indulge them.

An entire planet was counting on the success of this mission. Not just one stubborn deputy.

Make that two.

Chapter 20

REMY

Remy dashed toward Dreyla, holding Dr. Sanger's prosthetic hand aloft.

She shrank against the giant refrigerator. "What the hell, you cut it off? Jesus, Remy!"

He tossed the appendage toward her. Shrieking, she caught the hand and juggled it in her own. It took a moment for her face to relax, realization dawning on her.

"Oh," she said, inspecting the artificial palm.

"The fingerprints on it should match those on the lock," he explained.

Dreyla nodded, then placed the hand, palm side

down, onto the scanner. The display whirred quietly as a red line moved across the strange fingerprints. After a few seconds, the screen emitted a neon-green glow, and perhaps a second after that, the seal released, a soft, satisfying hiss emanating as the door slowly opened.

Dreyla grabbed the door handle, yanked it outward, and gestured toward the nans. "Ta-da!"

Remy immediately stepped inside the storage unit, headed for the nearest crate, and opened the lid.

"Jackpot," he breathed.

Until that moment, he hadn't let himself fully believe the meds were on the premises. No matter the universe, it always seemed to pull a fast one whenever he thought he'd achieved something of worth. But here lay thirty stacked rows of little white packages, each emblazoned with an official black-and-blue logo, and there sat twenty-three other crates just like this one.

"So," Dreyla said, snagging his attention.

He shut the lid, secured the hasp, and turned toward her, his eyebrow arched in anticipation.

"How are we getting out of here?" she asked, her expectant gaze fixed on his face. "We didn't discuss the details of that part."

Jacer's tall, slender frame appeared on the far side of the refrigeration unit. "I had assumed this building had a rear entrance." He glanced forlornly at the windowless corridor behind him. "We probably should have thought this out a bit better."

Remy grinned. "Lady Ris, are you and your ladies outside?"

"Yes, Captain," came the head monk's immediate, ever-serene response via the comms. *"We are in place."*

"Great." He turned to his companions. "OK, start carrying the crates into the hallway."

Dreyla's frown morphed into a half-smirk. "That's why you told the sheriff we'd make our own exit."

His grin widened. As usual, she'd grasped his crazy-ass plan.

She removed another roll of mesh from her satchel. "Want me to put a hole in the back wall?" she asked sweetly.

"Not yet," Remy replied. "It's a busy street. We don't know who else might be out there, even at this hour."

"Excuse me, Captain," Lady Ris politely interrupted.

"What is it?"

"We have an adequate view of the block, and it *is* a lot more crowded than I would have expected."

"Right, thanks." He turned to his two companions. "For now, get the mesh ready and start carting the boxes over to that spot."

With a nod, Dreyla zipped up her bag. Jacer, meanwhile, holstered his gun, walked into the cooler, and lifted one of the crates.

While the two of them got to work, Remy grabbed his own satchel and then sprinted through the storage room, down the corridor, and into the doctor's office, where Milo, Sheriff Greyson, and Deputy Davis huddled near the open doorway leading into the reception area, their firearms at the ready.

"What the hell?" Remy shouted. "I told you to secure that door."

"Brand's still out there," Davis whined. "What if she comes through the front?"

"That sucks," Remy said, "but sorry to say, we don't have time to wait for her. We need to hold this position just long enough to move the meds out."

The sheriff caught his gaze. Far from looking ecstatic over his drug-busting prowess, she eyed him incredulously. "Move them out? How?" She cocked her head toward the front entrance, which was still getting slammed with nerve-rattling blasts. "You're not serious about busting through the back?"

Remy shook his head, equally annoyed, then crept past the armed trio and headed toward the receptionist's massive desk. "Help me turn this thing on its side so we can use it for cover."

Milo stepped beside him, and together, the two of them pivoted the desk onto its side and slid it across the tiled floor, providing cover for the inner doorway.

"Thanks, Milo," Remy said. "Now, go help Jacer and Dreyla move the crates over to our exit point."

With a curt nod, the dworg trotted back into the doctor's office.

Lilly and Davis lingered in the open doorway, dodging a few wayward blasts.

"And you two idiots," Remy said, smirking, "get your asses down here with me. You're liable to get shot if you stay there."

Just as the sheriff and the deputy complied, Remy heard a series of thuds in the stairwell. Carefully, he leaned from behind the overturned desk, his blaster aimed at the door leading to the stairs.

Dr. Sanger burst into the reception area, his short, stocky body stuffed into a ridiculous vest and a pair of raggedy boxer shorts. Despite the cacophony of shouts and blasts in the courtyard, he remained near the front entrance, his face still aflame with anger and embarrassment, his hair sticking out in haphazard tufts. And that... alternative hand... still attached to his right wrist.

"You scum," Dr. Sanger snarled. "You'll pay for this. Wait until Mr. Darkbur gets his hands on you."

"I'd rather *his* hands than yours," Remy said wryly.

Davis peered above the desk. "Is—is that a *penis* on his hand?"

Ignoring him, the doctor twisted toward the front door, his left hand reaching for the handle.

"Don't even think about it," Remy warned.

The doctor shot him an obstinate glare over his shoulder, then slammed down on the handle. He hadn't even opened the door all the way before a barrage of blasts hit him in the face and torso. He was so riddled with bolts of plasma energy that his body almost vanished into a bloody mist.

"Holy crap," Lilly muttered beside Remy, her arms shielding her face from the nasty spray.

Remy unleashed a round of blasts through the open doorway, and his two cohorts followed suit. Two of Darkbur's men took fatal shots to the head as they attempted to rush inside, then someone else tossed a smoke grenade through the front entrance. Immediately, the room filled with a thick gray haze. Unable to discern the enemy, Remy continued firing at the doorway. With any luck, he'd hit anyone foolish enough to cross the threshold. Just hopefully not the sheriff's missing deputy.

"Davis, move back," Lilly shouted above the din. "Help the others transfer the crates."

Nodding, Davis crawled into the examination room, while Remy and Sheriff Greyson hunkered behind the desk and maintained a stalwart defense.

When Remy noticed his and the sheriff's plasma blasts ricocheting off some unseen barrier, he tossed his blaster aside and drew his trusty Colt again.

"Someone's put up a shield," Sheriff Greyson said, holstering her gun. She laid a restraining hand on his forearm. "It's no use, Captain."

He almost protested, but he knew she was right.

Sometimes, you gotta flee to fight another day.

Before he could agree with her, however, he heard Dreyla's voice over the comms.

"Captain, we're ready to go!"

"Burn it, Drey!" he yelled.

Then, with his hand on the small of the sheriff's back, he crouched low and pushed her firmly through the inner doorway. For once, she didn't protest.

Shielding himself behind the doorframe, he removed a plasma grenade from his satchel, tossed it toward the front entrance, and slammed the inner door shut.

Following the subsequent eruption in the reception area, the walls and the foundation of the three-story building quaked. Seconds later, Remy heard muffled screams of pain from the other side of the door.

Then, one booming, belligerent voice rose above the commotion.

"Go around," Darkbur ordered. "They're trying to escape out the back!"

Chapter
21

DREYLA

Dreyla stood guard beside the open hole in the rear wall of the building, her arm muscles tensed as she gripped her plasma blaster. Bolstered by her successful rooftop breach, she'd taken little time to create their escape route with her customized mesh, but now, she felt anxious again. She longed to help Milo, Jacer, and Davis, who were alternately stepping in and out of the hole, transferring the crates of nano-biotics from the corridor to the monks' waiting hovercrafts.

She peered around the nearest edge of the sizable hole. The planet's sun had started to rise a few minutes ago, and the streetlights had automatically turned off.

When she'd first activated the mesh and disintegrated part of the wall, she'd noticed a plethora of pedestrians on both sidewalks of the street behind the Butcher's Place. Bane seemed to sport heavy foot traffic at all hours, day or night, and even with the loud-ass commotion in the courtyard of Gono Darkbur's property, the thoroughfare had teemed with humans, aflins, dworgs, and other unclassified passersby. Once Darkbur's men had circled around the building, though, and a firefight had ensued beyond the borders of the crime lord's property, the street had cleared faster than Drey could say *showdown.*

Remy hurried toward her, frowning. "They're gonna hit us on the street."

"They already are, Cap." She cocked her head toward the scene outside.

At that exact moment, plasma blasts shot past the hole in both directions, clearly demonstrating her point.

Remy's frown deepened, and so did the sheriff's behind him.

Jacer stepped back inside the hallway to grab another crate. Spotting Remy, Dreyla, and Lilly, he said, "Lady Ris and her people are trying to hold off Darkbur's men, but there are just too many of them."

Grimacing, Remy edged toward the doctor's office and glanced at the closed door leading to the reception area. "At least no one will be coming through that way...

for a while anyway."

He turned back to Jacer, who had remained standing near the open hole with a crate balanced on his forearms, as if awaiting new instructions.

"I tossed a plasma grenade that likely took out a few of them," Remy elaborated.

"That explains the minor earthquake I felt," Jacer remarked.

Remy smirked. "But it won't take them long to figure out we're not defending the front anymore. So, just finish stowing the crates. We need to get outta here as soon as we can."

Davis ducked back inside to grab another container. "You're telling me. It's getting pretty dicey out there." He lifted a crate, then paused. "And we still have to find Brand."

No one replied to his statement, not with reassurances or protests. Not even the sheriff.

Dreyla's gaze shifted from her companions to the street outside. The large explosion Remy had set off in the reception area might've killed a few of Darkbur's men, and some of them had surely died from various bullets and blasts, but she had no idea how many of their enemies Remy, Lilly, and the others had eliminated. From the looks of the mayhem in the street, Gono Darkbur wasn't running out of bad guys anytime soon.

Davis and Jacer, each carrying a crate, edged toward the hole, but before they could make their death-defying dash to the hovercrafts, a harried Milo darted inside, ducking several plasma streaks.

"Holy Yerdua," the dworg shouted. "It's sheer madness out there!"

Lilly's forehead crinkled with concern. "What should we do?"

A rare moment of indecision for the sheriff, but, given the raging skirmish outside, Drey couldn't really blame her.

"A couple of us need to finish hauling out the crates," Remy suggested, "while the rest provide some cover for them."

He stepped toward the hole, grabbed the seared edge, and stuck his head outside. Before Dreyla could yell at him for being an impulsive idiot, he retracted his head and gave her a long, hard stare, his jaws clenched tightly. He was obviously sizing up the danger level, as he always did when she was involved. She wanted to tell him not to bother—that she could handle anything he could—but the words wouldn't budge from her throat.

No matter what option Remy took, the probability of death had hit the stratosphere. People on both sides of the battle were shooting haphazardly in every direction.

Drey found it hard to fathom escaping this mess un-scathed.

The one advantage in their favor was that Lady Ris and her fellow monks had parked their three hovercrafts between two large transport vehicles, providing limited cover from shooters on either end of the street. Unfortunately, blasts were also coming from above them, indicating that some of Darkbur's men had taken elevated positions in the hotel or perhaps even on the roof of the rear building.

Dreyla certainly didn't need Remy to tell her any of this. She'd worked out the angles and the odds all on her own, leading to one inevitable conclusion: They were royally screwed.

"Stay here," he said. "Keep a count on the crates. We need them *all*."

She opened her mouth to object when another twangy blast shot past the hole in the wall, followed by a female scream of anguish. Dreyla's heart thumped as she instinctively peered outside.

"Oh, no. Not again."

One of Darkbur's gunmen had apparently blown off the arm of one of Lady Ris's fellow monks. The afflicted woman bent forward, clutching her bloody shoulder, a dark stain rapidly spreading across her diaphanous robe. Two of the other ladies, jabbering urgently, dragged her to the nearest hovercraft.

It unsettled Dreyla to witness such a horrendous injury befall such an incredible woman—just as it had during the bloody raid in Trame. Since visiting the monastery, she had pictured all the Ladies of Morbious as perfect, impervious, immortal beings that inhabited a celestial dimension where only good things happened, but as it turned out, they were just as vulnerable—and mortal—as anyone else.

Remy's eyes darkened. "OK, that's it. We can't delay. Milo, Jacer, finish loading the rest of the crates. Davis, Lilly, and I will try to keep the bastards busy." He turned to Dreyla and handed her his equipment bag. "You hang back and shoot anyone not on our side."

Remy, Lilly, and Davis checked their weapons and then dispersed into the street, zigzagging through the plasma blasts and searching for ideal shooting spots. With stalwart expressions, Milo and Jacer stepped outside with the nineteenth and twentieth crates and bolted toward the hovercrafts. The uninjured monks, meanwhile, struggled to defend their position. Dreyla felt torn between wanting to help speed up the loading process and obey her father's command to stay put.

"Ooowww," Jacer keened in his high-pitched voice.

The aflin, who had just deposited his latest crate, sank to the sidewalk beside one of the hovercrafts. A blast had seemingly caught his left hip. Milo hastened to help him to his feet, and then, partially covered by the monks' gunfire, the two unlikely pals staggered down the sidewalk, through the busted wall, and into the doctor's office.

Dreyla abandoned her post and raced to Jacer's side. "Are you alright?"

The aflin's wound oozed a strange greenish fluid (probably just his blood) that made the injury look more gruesome than it likely was. Jacer leaned against the exam table in the middle of the cluttered room, grimacing in pain, but closer scrutiny indicated the wound was little more than a graze.

"I'll be OK," Jacer said, waving her and Milo away.

With an amiable shrug, the dworg returned to the hallway to grab another crate. A few seconds later, the aflin straightened up and followed suit, and Dreyla resumed her post. As she kept watch, the men lugged two more heavy containers—numbers twenty-one and twenty-two—out into the melee, apparently ignoring the injuries they'd already sustained and seemingly immune to the blasts shooting past their heads. Davis, Lilly, and Remy, meanwhile, continued to assist the monks in keeping the gunmen at bay.

Left alone again, Dreyla hunkered beside the hole,

just inside the corridor, and tried to find an ideal position. One that allowed her to shoot any enemies on the sidewalk and still conceal herself behind the wall—thus being useful *and* adhering to Remy's order to stay safe. From where she crouched, she spied a trio of Darkbur's men headed toward the hovercrafts, so she aimed her pistol, pulled the trigger, and... missed.

Crap.

Yeah, she'd rarely been proficient with handguns, especially from a distance. She would've brought her trusty plasma crossbow instead, but Remy had thought it would draw too much attention—back when the plan had been to slip in and out like an unseen wind.

Ha! As if that's ever the case with us.

Now, she wished she hadn't listened to him. What did drawing undue attention matter anymore? Hell, even shooting one of Remy's old-time gunpowder guns would be easier than this stupid blaster.

Despite the high-tech nature of the blasters, the old-fashioned firearms—*cowboy guns*, Tosh called them—were actually faster, more accurate shots in the right hands. But that wasn't why Remy preferred them. They were simply part of his fixation with ancient artifacts. His .45 Colt wasn't even a proper gunpowder weapon. She'd had to fabricate special bullets for him. But it still fired as well as it had two hundred years ago.

Or so Remy claims.

The aflin and the dworg darted back in and out so quickly that Dreyla only caught a glimpse of Milo's new injury—on his right shoulder. Before she could even consider worrying, she heard a ruckus in the reception area. Apparently, some of Darkbur's men had noted the stillness on that side of the closed door and decided to breach their hidey-hole from behind.

Dammit!

All the crates were gone. It was time for her to go, but she wasn't sure where. Between the haphazard plasma blasts and the irritating haze from several grenades, she found it difficult to see much from her position. Hands shaking, she lifted the blaster again, squinted through the hole in the wall, and fired at a nebulous figure lurking under a streetlamp. Unfortunately, the shot sailed way over the gunman's head.

She grunted in frustration.

Well, if Remy could indulge his nostalgic whims about guns, then next time, she would bring her damn crossbow.

If there even *was* a next time.

Chapter 22

REMY

This situation felt like déjà vu of the worst kind. Remy gazed toward the middle hovercraft, where the stricken monk still bled profusely, and his stomach swirled. The woman struggled to constrain her cries of agony as Bellia and Lady Ris wrapped bandages around the shoulder area and dabbed her face with cloths. Overcome with frenzied concern, they had switched to some other language he'd never heard before.

The poor woman had lost her entire right arm, just like Commander Shaw had... only in Shaw's case, it had been an act of desperation on Remy's part. An effort to save his daughter from an unacceptable demise. But these monsters—Gono Darkbur's goons—were willing to maim and kill as many people as necessary, just to reclaim the drugs they'd stolen from everyone on the planet. They were the most heinous scum imaginable, on par with Larker Max.

Remy didn't make a habit of letting people steal back what he'd rightfully stolen, particularly when the loot in question had been originally stolen from others.

What a confusing mess. A whole lotta stealing going on.

One thing was certain, though: He and his companions were doing the right thing—for a lot of innocent and, yes, some not-so-innocent people on Vox. Remy didn't usually stick his neck out for anyone other than the *Jay*'s crew, whom he considered family, but this situation had pissed him off enough to relax his principles.

Someone grabbed his elbow and yanked him into the gap between the nearest hovercraft and one of the humongous transport vehicles that bookended the trio of monk-driven vessels, just as a half-dozen shots whizzed by, narrowly missing his nose. In the light of the rising sun, he could easily make out his rescuer.

"Are you crazy?" Sheriff Greyson yelled into his

face, her eyes flashing with fury. "Is that your problem?"

He winked at her. "Maybe just a wee bit."

Her glare only intensified. Apparently, she wasn't in a laughing mood. Her black hair was a tangled mess, and her right cheek bore a streak of blood. Given the strength and energy she radiated, Remy suspected it was someone else's. He glanced downward as she checked her weapons. She had abandoned her plasma rifle and was now sporting two pistols, aiming to shoot double-handed.

Yeah, he knew the real reason he was fighting this particular fight.

She caught his eye again with her fiery gaze. "We need to get the hell out of here!"

"No kidding."

He risked a look around the transport vehicle and glanced down the sidewalk. Half a dozen men rapidly advanced toward the hovercrafts. They needed to halt these scumbags, but unfortunately, most of their people had shifted their focus to repelling the attack from the street and the rooftops. Not the sidewalk.

Remy turned back to the sheriff and reached into one of her jacket pockets.

"What the hell are you—"

"Relax, Sheriff."

He pulled out the plasma wall cube, activated it, and hurled it down the sidewalk. The cube tumbled past

Darkbur's property and came to a halt several yards beyond the transport vehicle.

Remy met the sheriff's gaze as the countdown began.

"That was the only one I had, you pickpocket," she said.

"Yeah. Sorry."

"Sure hope you know what you're doing."

"Always."

She rolled her eyes, in a manner that would've made Dreyla proud.

Remy peered around the hovercraft and spotted Davis peeking out from beside the other transport vehicle. Taking the hint, the deputy activated his own grenade and tossed it toward the opposite end of the sidewalk.

Any second now, Remy's cube would form a barrier not far from the lead vehicle.

Ah, there it is.

The shimmering, white-hot plasma wall shot up and out, temporarily halting the gunmen charging toward them. The goons only had enough room between the edge of the plasma wall and Darkbur's property to enter the fray in single file. Milo and two of the monks easily took down the men.

Davis, unfortunately, had thrown his grenade too far to the left, where it bounced against Darkbur's building. The one Dreyla still hid inside.

Remy and Lilly winced at each other.

"That's not good," Lilly said.

"Nope, not good," Remy agreed.

He slid his arm around her waist and pulled her toward him. Instead of shaking him off, as in the recent past, she huddled beside him.

When, after several tense seconds, Davis's grenade finally ignited, the unleashed plasma wall sliced into the building, which promptly burst into flames. The other end of the wall luckily hit one of Darkbur's men, burning the side of his face. Shouting in pain, he rolled to the ground but still managed to raise his pistol.

By the time the thug squeezed his trigger, Remy knew Davis was a dead man. The deputy, who now stood on the sidewalk, staring agape at the fire he'd started, took a shot straight to the chest. Right through the light armor he wore beneath his shirt. He slumped to the ground, motionless.

"Nooooo!" the sheriff screamed.

She broke away from Remy and started to rise, but he pulled her back to safety just as a barrage of blasts exploded from both ends of the sidewalk. Instinctively, they each scurried backward and fell against Jacer, who, unbeknownst to them, had slipped into the space between vehicles. He'd been hit again, this time in the forearm. After noting the injury, Remy opened his mouth to say something, but the aflin simply shook his head, as if warding off any inquiries.

"Crates are all loaded," he said. "Ready to go."

"Wonderful," Remy replied. "Now, we just need to survive the battle long enough to escape."

He stood cautiously, assisted the teary-eyed sheriff to her feet as well, and then glanced back at the man sporting the gruesomely charred face, the one who'd killed Deputy Davis. As the man turned his gun toward the burning building, Remy traced his line of sight and spotted a shell-shocked Dreyla crouching on the other side of the breached wall. Clearly upset over Davis's murder and perhaps rattled by the rapidly spreading fire, she didn't realize how vulnerable she was.

"Drey!" Remy hollered. "Get back!"

As he watched helplessly from his hiding spot, an arm reached from behind her and yanked her farther into the building, just as the man's blasts flew through the hole.

Remy sighed with relief but then, a second later, found himself wondering who had just saved his daughter. Had Deputy Brand made it safely through the burning wreckage of the reception area?

With cold, clear tunnel vision, Remy leapt onto the sidewalk and sprinted toward the hole. Something hard knocked him off his path, making him stagger backward. It was Milo, barreling past him—or, rather, through him—to reach the scarred man who'd shot Davis.

Before the man, who towered over Milo, had a chance to defend himself, the dworg picked him up and, with a guttural roar, slammed him repeatedly against the sidewalk. Even with the din of shouting, gunfire, explosions, and raging flames all around him, Remy could swear he heard the man's skull and backbone crack under the pressure. When Milo seemed satisfied, he stumbled past the corpse and scooped up Davis's body, gamely taking another shot to his side as if it were a mere mosquito bite.

Rapidly spreading flames now engulfed much of Darkbur's building, formerly home to the twisted Dr. Sanger. Remy's focus yo-yoed between the smoke-filled hole where Drey had disappeared and the sheriff, still standing between the vehicles, both guns cocked.

This was it. Their time was up.

Chapter 23

DREYLA

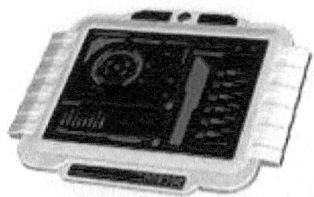

After stumbling backward—and watching in horror as several plasma blasts arced over her head and pierced the corner of the corridor—Dreyla instinctively turned to see who'd pulled her away from the outer wall.

What the hell?

Not believing her own eyes, she did a double take. But she'd been right the first time.

Backlit by the open doorway of the blazing reception area, and surrounded by a slew of the mad doctor's assorted body parts, stood Commander Tara Shaw—in all her svelte, black-suited, bionic-bitchin' glory.

Drey retreated a few steps, and Shaw followed her back into the hallway.

"You should be more careful, little one," she said, her green eyes alight with mischief.

Dreyla gazed speechlessly into the woman's porcelain face, Shaw's delicate features slightly marred by fresh scratches and bruises.

"But... you want to kill us," she blubbered.

"No." With her menacing cyborg arm, Shaw motioned to a spot beyond Dreyla. "Just him."

Dreyla followed her piercing gaze toward the rectangular hole in the rear wall, where Remy crouched on the sidewalk, staring at his longtime enemy.

"Like a bad penny, Shaw," Remy said, resting his Colt on his thigh, "you always seem to turn up."

Dreyla's mind raced, trying to think of a way to diffuse the situation. As she turned back to Shaw, though, she froze. The woman had raised her pistol in the captain's direction, a twisted smile on her lips.

Dreyla shifted her gaze back to Remy, mentally begging him to dive out of the way, but he merely lifted a forefinger, gestured to something behind her, and broadened his cocky grin.

Shaw whirled around, but before she could shift her gun and switch targets, the butt of a rifle hit her square in the forehead. She swayed for a moment, then collapsed at Dreyla's feet, her pistol slipping from her grasp.

Gasping, Dreyla looked up from the prone commander. With merciless eyes, the beefy, square-jawed assailant who'd knocked out Shaw flipped his rifle around and aimed the deadly end downward, directly at Dreyla's face. Apparently, he didn't mind sparing Shaw's life—likely because they worked for the same boss—but he had no intention of doing the same for Dreyla.

Before the gunman could squeeze the trigger, though, two bullets hit him in the left temple, spraying blood and brain matter out the other side of his head. His rifle clattered to the floor, and the dead man slumped heavily beside the unconscious commander.

Whoa, that was close. Too close.

With her blood still pounding in her ears, Dreyla pivoted toward the hole. Remy still crouched there, his favorite gun held aloft. When his eyes met his daughter's, he exhaled heavily and lowered his shoulders. Dreyla sighed, too, having momentarily forgotten how to breathe.

"*Remy... Dreyla,*" Lady Ris said via the comms, her tone more breathless than usual. "*Everyone is aboard. It is time to go.*"

"Get your ass out here," he growled at Dreyla.

"We're leaving!"

He didn't have to tell her twice. The fire had already found its way into the doctor's former office, incinerating everything in its path and making a mockery of the overhead sprinklers, which only managed to spray a pathetic mist of useless water. Flames licked the floor, edging toward the corridor. The pinkish-gray smoke billowing toward the ceiling was probably highly toxic, and it smelled terrible. Like burning rubber, seared flesh, and pungent chemicals all blended as one.

Dreyla sprang toward the outer wall, grabbing her and Remy's satchels along the way. A series of explosions throughout the structure made the inner walls tremble and crack. The building wasn't long for this particular world, and neither was anyone trapped inside.

Well, crap.

Halting at the open hole in the wall, she ignored Remy's extended hand and glanced backward at the two bodies behind her. As her gaze drifted from the dead man to the unconscious commander, she sighed.

"Dammit, Drey," she muttered.

Without further hesitation, she tossed the bags toward her father, darted to the open doorway of Dr. Sanger's former office, grabbed Shaw's arms, and dragged her through the hole and onto the sidewalk. Luckily, the woman didn't weigh much more than Dreyla did.

Additional eruptions sounded from inside the building, and the heat of the engulfing fire roasted Dreyla's skin. So, with her last ounces of energy, she lugged the commander into the street, where it was slightly cooler. As she finally released Shaw's arms, she looked up and met the captain's uncomprehending eyes. Although he'd been quick enough to step aside as Dreyla pulled Shaw out of harm's way, he certainly didn't seem pleased.

"What the hell are you *doing*?" he asked.

"She saved my life," Dreyla reasoned, although she couldn't really justify what she'd done, even to herself. "Said she only wanted to kill you." She shrugged. "I mean, I'm not happy about that, but still, it seemed wrong to leave her behind."

Remy said nothing for a long moment, then shrugged, too. "Fair enough. But she's not coming with us."

He grasped Dreyla's arm and nearly dragged her toward the trio of waiting hovercrafts, where their crewmates were still firing at Darkbur's men. The temporary plasma walls had disappeared, but the furnace created by the collapsing building had helped to keep some of the bad guys preoccupied. It would only take a few well-aimed plasma blasts, though, to overwhelm the good guys and re-store Darkbur's diabolical control over the backwater planet.

Remy and Dreyla reached the nearest hovercraft. Lady Ris and Sheriff Lilly sat in the vehicle, putting up an admirable fight, alternately ducking from plasma blasts and firing their own pistols at the goons clustered at both ends of the street. But their shots merely bounced off their formidable body armor.

Remy took aim with his Colt and ripped a hole through the armored chest of one of the thugs, who crum-pled to the ground. The dead man's fellow assassins hesi-tated just long enough for Dreyla and Remy to scramble inside the hovercraft.

Yay for old-school tech! And my special bullets.

Then, amid the roar of flames and a spray of plasma blasts, Remy took the wheel, guided the hovercraft into the street, and steered them away from the terrifying scene. Crouching in the passenger seat, Dreyla turned to watch the mayhem behind her. Lilly and Lady Ris were still shooting, trying to provide cover for the other two open-topped hovercrafts, which had successfully escaped as well.

Dreyla's gaze shifted to the left, where the fire now

engulfed the rear building—truly a lost cause. Worse, a few flames had hopped to the adjacent hotel, where they licked the lower floors. She wouldn't feel guilty if Gono Darkbur lost his entire property, but she hoped the hotel guests and bar patrons had had the good sense to flee.

"Get down," Remy urged her, pressing his palm on the crown of her head.

Dreyla obeyed, crouching as low as she could in the footwell. After what she'd just endured, she didn't have the will to argue. As much as she longed to help the others, she wasn't sure she could hold a gun steady enough to avoid shooting one of her own teammates, much less hit any of the bad guys.

Remy whipped the hovercraft around a sharp corner, which elicited murmurs of alarm from Lilly and Lady Ris—as well as mingled protests from the other two vehicles.

"Where are you going?" the sheriff demanded.

"We need to get our man," Remy growled.

Via his earpiece comms, he tried to raise Tosh, but got no answer.

Dreyla gasped in the small, cramped space below the passenger seat. She'd nearly forgotten about Tosh. She'd just assumed he was OK, but how could he be? They'd left him on the twelfth floor of a hotel that was now on fire. The captain obviously intended to circle around the property and liberate the doc through the non-burning side of the Butcher's Place.

Even from the footwell, she could see her fellow passengers. While Lilly had remained in the back of the hovercraft, sitting among several strapped-down crates of nano-biotics, firing at the gunmen chasing them below, Lady Ris had shifted her weapon toward the front of the vehicle.

Oh, great. Hostiles coming at us from both directions.

But after the captain's pronouncement, the sheriff paused in her firing and whipped her head toward the driver's seat.

"Negative," she said coldly. "A third of the shipment's on board this craft."

"Well, I'm not leaving Tosh behind," he replied, a stubborn note in his voice.

Dreyla knew he would tolerate no further discussion.

"You are, Bechet," Lilly said in a voice as unbending as the captain's. "Look, I've lost two deputies over this, and for all I know, Brand's dead, too. I don't want to lose her either, but we've got no choice. Too many lives are at stake."

"Captain," Lady Ris intervened, "it really would be more prudent to leave this area."

As always, the head monk sounded cool, calm, and collected. She'd even continued shooting at Darkbur's men while she spoke. Unfortunately, her wise advice wouldn't benefit Tosh.

"Besides," Lady Ris continued, "two of my ladies went back to retrieve him."

Although Dreyla felt slightly relieved by this news, Remy's pulsing jaw made it clear he was less than convinced. The captain never liked leaving anything important in other people's hands.

Stretching upward and peering through the windshield, Dreyla could see people running for cover in the streets. Hard to believe that anyone not on Darkbur's payroll had stayed in the area.

"We need to get out of Bane!" the sheriff yelled desperately. "Turn around, Bechet. Now."

"Not gonna happen," Remy yelled back. "I'm not leaving Tosh."

"Yes, you are." The sheriff's voice had turned intractable again—and ice-cold.

Abandoning caution, Dreyla clambered onto the passenger's seat for a better look. Having concealed the hovercraft behind a nearby building, Remy had turned his head to meet the sheriff's stony gaze with a similarly humorless expression of his own. The sheriff had shifted her gun, now pointing it directly at Remy's head.

"You're going to shoot me?" he asked, his tone resigned but his eyes flashing, as if daring her to pull the trigger.

"If I have to," the sheriff snapped. "If this shipment gets destroyed or taken back to Darkbur, a lot of those that need the meds will be dead in weeks. Maybe even days." She exhaled nervously, tossing back her dark, disheveled hair. "Please, Remy."

To the untrained eye, the captain's face remained immobile, but Dreyla noted the miniscule patches of pink blooming below his cheekbones, not to mention a tiny muscle twitching near his left jaw. She'd seen that look before, and it usually meant trouble.

"She is right, Captain Bechet," Lady Ris implored, lowering her weapon. "We cannot go back there. You must turn around."

Remy glanced at the monk, then over at Dreyla, then back at the dashboard. The fact that he *didn't* look at the sheriff made Drey's chest tighten. A bad omen indeed.

He wrenched down on a lever and gunned the hovercraft into a stomach-churning turn, his hands clamped on the steering wheel, his knuckles white, his face rigid.

Dreyla's head buzzed. She knew why he'd turned

around. Not to save the people of Vox.

No, he'd done it because he'd chosen *that woman* over Tosh.

Hot tears streaked down her cheeks as the vessel rocked back and forth. Listlessly, she heard yelling in the streets and saw plasma blasts sailing past the hovercraft, but she hardly cared about the danger.

A blur of minutes later, Dreyla registered an ear-splitting crash as the captain busted through the city gates, which, to be fair, looked mangled already. Hopefully, the other two hovercrafts had made it out safely.

Soon afterward, they were gliding across a wide-open desert, far from the city, where the air was slightly cooler and infinitely fresher. In the distance, she could discern the other two vehicles waiting for them. Although she felt relieved to see them, dismay and dread still plagued her heart. Dreyla twisted around in her seat and gazed back at the buildings of Bane in the early-morning light. As they diminished in size, she wondered if she'd ever see Tosh again.

She turned around in her seat and shot the captain a dirty look, but he ignored her—and everyone else— merely pretending to focus on his driving.

"What's the likelihood they'll chase us?" the sheriff asked Lady Ris.

"Oh, I am certain they will try to," she replied, "but

we will have air support within thirty minutes. There are half a dozen mini-wings headed our way, and my ladies are excellent pilots."

Dreyla didn't know what the hell *mini-wings* were, but somehow, she trusted they'd be good enough to cover the rest of their escape.

Well, they'd better be.

Of course, Darkbur didn't strike Dreyla as the type of criminal to lose a battle gracefully. If anything like Larker Max, he wouldn't stop until he'd reclaimed every last crate. And given the destruction zone back at the Butcher's Place, he certainly wouldn't balk at retaliating on the sheriff's station in Naillik, much less a monastery. Especially since he'd already attacked said holy place.

For now, though, Dreyla merely sank into her seat, folded her arms across her chest, and thought of Tosh... the crazy, lovable old man, all alone. The man who, in a heartbeat, would've given up his own life for either Dreyla or Remy.

A fresh tear rolled down her face, but before her father noticed, she wiped it away with her fist.

Chapter 24

SHAW

Amid agonizing throbs, unbearable heat, and deafening roars and screams, Shaw regained consciousness. As her eyelids fluttered open, she considered her immediate situation. She lay on her back on the hard ground, staring at a lightening sky filled with acrid, hellish smoke.

What the hell's going on?

One thing was certain: Shaw was tired of being

knocked unconscious, only to wake up aching and confused in a strange, unwelcome place, especially after missing yet another chance to execute Captain Remy Bechet. Besides a sizable headache and a tender welt on her forehead, though, she seemed relatively intact.

Gingerly, she sat upright and looked around.

Nope, not strange after all.

In fact, she recognized the scene. She was sitting in the street behind the Butcher's Place. Only, everything was on fire. The rear building as well as the main structure housing the saloon, brothel, and hotel were all ablaze and crumbling to the ground with loud, protesting moans.

"What a crapstorm," said a deep, familiar voice beside her.

She turned to the side and noticed Darius standing alone in the street. Covered in black body armor and armed to the hilt, he looked as sexy as ever.

He turned to her, his grim, hardened face still one of the most handsome things she'd seen since crashing on Vox. She attempted a smile, but it hurt her own face too much.

Glancing toward both ends of the empty street and noting several bodies on the sidewalks, she could only guess that the rest of Darkbur's troops had either chased after Bechet and his people, slipped away to lick their wounds, or died during the battle over the meds. But Darius was a survivor, like her, so it didn't surprise her to see him standing here, with little more than a sweaty brow for his trouble.

The last thing she could remember was standing in a now-burning medical laboratory, facing one of Darkbur's gunmen. After she got knocked out yet again, Darius must have spotted her lying on the floor and pulled her away from the encroaching flames.

Gazing back at the thunderous inferno, she said, "Thanks for getting me out of there."

"I didn't."

She met his unyielding gaze again.

Huh. Must have been the kid then. Imagine that.

Cautiously, she rose to her feet, dusted the ash from her uniform, and tucked several strands of limp, dampened hair behind her ears.

Just then, the rear wall of the building buckled under the pressure, and the upper levels collapsed amid a geyser of smoke and flame. Instinctively, Shaw and Darius took a few steps backward.

"Your boss isn't going to be happy about this," she remarked, surveying the damage.

"He's not." Darius held up the tiny comms unit he'd removed from his ear—probably after Darkbur had screamed holy hell at him. "By the way, he's your boss as well. And he's especially pissed at you."

She performed a quick search for her weapons, but found she was unarmed. Again. And the earpiece she'd swiped from that deputy was gone, too.

Glancing downward, she spotted a small pile of familiar-looking blades and guns on the ground, not far from Darius's feet.

Noting her companion's clenched jaw and merciless eyes, she squinted with suspicion. "Did you take my weapons?"

"You're not gonna need them," he said calmly.

In that moment, she realized that her favorite drinking companion was no longer on her side. If given the chance, he probably would have left her in the burning building. Since one of Darkbur's men had knocked her out, the crime lord had undoubtedly issued a *kill-or-capture* order. Having lost one of his businesses and perhaps the meds as well, Darkbur was likely in no mood for her shenanigans or excuses—and he needed someone beyond Captain Bechet and Sheriff Greyson to blame, especially if they were currently out of reach.

Of course, what both Darkbur and Darius failed to realize was that Shaw would never succumb without a fight. Gono Darkbur and his minions weren't used to dealing with truly competent quarry... or lucky ones.

"Sorry," she said, and actually meant it.

"Apologies aren't going to help—" Darius began, lifting his blaster in her direction.

"I know." An unabashed grin spread across her face as she glanced beyond him. "But I'm still sorry."

Before he could decide whether or not to turn around, the driver's-side door of a fast-moving hovercraft slammed into his back, sending him sprawling facedown to the ground.

Shaw stepped aside just in time, as the vehicle came to an immediate halt a few paces away.

Zain's head swiveled toward her. "Commander."

Jibs, sitting beside his cohort, grinned like a bloody fool.

She'd never been so pleased to see her two subordinates. Not that she planned to tell them so.

"Nice ride," she said as she stepped over Darius and circled around to the passenger side.

"It's gonna be a bit tight in here." Jibs opened the door and scooted over. "I think this thing was made for two."

She gazed down at Darius, who stirred on the ground below. He lifted his head slowly, and his dark eyes locked with hers, his expression both hurt and confused.

Well, you were ready to shoot me.

"Like I said…" She edged toward him. "Sorry."

As she crouched next to him, her right fist collided with his face, the unyielding alloy crunching bones under its immense force. His head hit the ground, where he remained in a motionless heap.

"Commander," Zain said urgently, "please get in the vehicle. We have to go."

After gathering her weapons, Shaw lifted herself into the hovercraft, squeezed onto the cramped seat, and slammed the door shut.

Bye, Darius. It's been fun.

Zain floored the accelerator and zoomed past the raging fire, making her jostle against Jibs.

"Sorry, Tara," Zain said, punching the thrust stabilizers.

She gazed past Jibs and stared at Zain's profile. In all the time he'd worked for her, he had never dared to call her by her first name. Some might have considered it insubordinate to do so now, but the funny thing was… he hadn't said it with disrespect in his tone, just simple familiarity.

Yes, she and her two crewmen were in this mess together. So, she'd let her number one call her Tara... at least until they managed to return to their own solar system.

Zain turned toward her, his mouth slowly morphing into an amiable grin.

"Wipe that smile off your face," she ordered.

Zain shifted forward again, his face resuming its default passivity as if nothing had happened.

With a tiny smile of her own, she stared through the windshield. Despite her pounding head, she surveyed their surroundings as they traveled across the city of Bane. Charred buildings still burned, and nasty-smelling smoke swirled everywhere. Sirens wailed, and sporadic plasma blasts streaked across the hazy sky. Citizens ran helter-skelter in and out of various structures, alternately yelling and crying.

Bechet and his crew must have caused at least some of the wreckage they presently glided through. It was his trademark, after all.

Maybe she'd get another shot at him, or maybe she should just cut her losses and leave him on this sickening dump of a planet. Darkbur would nail him one way or another, and the arrogant crime lord likely had an assortment of creative torture methods at his disposal.

No matter what, though, she and her guys needed to get to Naillik and jack that med ship ASAP.

A bunch of armed guards attempted to stop them at the mangled gates, but amid a volley of plasma blasts, Zain simply ducked his head and crashed right through the compromised barrier. He'd totally read her mind. Another sign of his intuition and common sense, for which she was exceedingly grateful. Her head, after all, throbbed too damn much for her to take control of the situation.

"If my calculations are accurate," Zain announced, "we'll reach Naillik in eight hours." He tightened his grip on the steering wheel. "If this piece of crap can make it that long," he added under his breath.

"It will," Shaw muttered in reply. "Then we grab that med ship and get off this damn planet."

She gazed ahead, across miles and miles of sand, boulders, and tumbleweeds, toward the golden horizon. She didn't want to be on-planet anymore. Living and working on the move, preferably in a starship of her own, suited her autonomous personality a whole lot better. Hell, she even got jittery on the mining asteroids, and the luxury space stations held no appeal for her whatsoever.

Open space, and a pirate to chase—that was how she liked it.

Chapter 25

LILLY

During the ride across the vast desert, Lilly edged her way toward the front of the hovercraft, crouched behind the passenger seat, and, while pretending to focus on the proximity scanner on the dashboard, snatched glances at Remy Bechet. The strain showed on the pirate's face—his squinting eyes, his clenched jaw, and the tiny blood vessel throbbing on his right temple. But given his steady expression, his black, silver-flecked hair flying in the wind, and his forearm muscles tightening as he clutched the wheel, she couldn't deny the flicker of attraction thawing her deep inside.

He'd succumbed to her demand. He'd turned around at gunpoint, leaving Tosh behind—a decision that must have deeply pained him.

A lump formed in her throat. She wanted to explain that she never would have shot him—that she'd only aimed her weapon out of sheer desperation for the people of Vox.

But then she noticed Bechet's face. He'd shifted his gaze toward Dreyla, and the obvious look of fatherly love and concern told her everything: He hadn't left behind the doctor for her or anyone else on this planet. He'd done it to get his daughter out of harm's way.

A peripheral flash alerted her, and she flicked her eyes back to the scanner.

"Uh-oh," Bechet said. "We've got company."

Apparently, he'd spotted the four incoming ships, too.

Lilly turned toward the back of the vehicle, planning to fire the rear blasters, but she knew they couldn't possibly fight off all the vessels at once, even with the other two hovercrafts. None of them sported the defenses that Darkbur's armed pursuers likely had.

"They have come," Lady Ris said, her eyes glowing with relief.

Confused by her expression, Lilly said, "Yes, I know."

"No, not Darkbur's people," Lady Ris replied, pointing westward. "The mini-wings."

Lilly followed her gaze, but she couldn't see anything with the naked eye. She turned back to the dashboard and spotted six dots on the scanner, swooping toward the four ships currently pursuing the trio of hovercrafts filled with the planet's entire supply of nano-biotics. Once the well-armed mini-wings appeared in the sky, Darkbur's ships turned around and headed back to Bane. Presumably, his men had calculated the odds and decided to give up the fight.

For now.

"Nice timing," Bechet said.

"One less worry," Lilly agreed.

The time passed uneventfully, but just as they were within sight of Trame, the hovercraft wobbled. Lilly glanced toward the front. Bechet's hands had slackened off the wheel.

What's he playing at?

Then he slumped forward, and the hovercraft veered dangerously off course.

Lilly made a dive for the steering wheel, but Dreyla

beat her to it. After pushing the captain back, the girl grasped the wheel and yanked it to the side, just in time to avoid plummeting over a cliff that overlooked and partially sheltered Trame. Dreyla hovered over Bechet's lap as she tried to guide the craft toward the monastery.

"What's wrong with him?" Lilly asked as she tugged Bechet towards her.

Once free of the driver's seat, the captain slumped backward onto the floor of the hovercraft. Murmuring incoherently, he didn't budge as Lilly undid the buttons of his dark-brown shirt. She assumed he'd been injured during the battle and stubbornly refused to inform anyone, Dreyla included. Glancing upward, Lilly spotted Dreyla in the driver's seat, trying to keep one eye on the path ahead and the other on Bechet.

"Is he OK?" she asked, her face filled with worry.

Lilly shrugged and resumed her inspection.

"Where does it hurt, Remy?" she asked, surveying his torso. "Are you losing blood?"

"Urrgh... Tosh," he mumbled.

As Lady Ris removed a first-aid kit from a side compartment, Lilly laid the back of her hand on Bechet's forehead. Feverish. Then, as she unfastened the last two buttons of his shirt, she noticed an increasingly large blood pool across his abdomen, almost at his waistline.

"Where's he hit?" Dreyla asked in a frenzy, alternately glancing between Lilly and the windshield.

Any anger and dismay the girl had felt over Bechet's decision to leave Bane without Tosh had fled. Now, she only had concern for her father.

"Looks like he was shot in the lower abdomen," Lilly said.

She grabbed the gauze Lady Ris had offered and applied pressure to the wound as Dreyla accelerated to the craft's top speed.

By the time they pulled into the complex, the Ladies of Morbious were waiting with their medical staff. Lilly had never felt so grateful to be in the presence of skilled doctors and nurses, even if they were all wearing the customary monastic garb of bikinis and robes.

Everyone on Lilly's team sported wounds, but Jacer, Milo, and Bechet were in the worst condition. While several monks guided or carted the wounded inside the medical outbuilding, Lilly asked Bellia about Piper, the monk who'd lost her arm in the battle.

"Sadly, she did not survive the journey home."

"Oh," Lilly said, "I'm so sorry."

"We lost Sienna, too."

Lilly's eyes teared—and not from the hot desert wind. She felt guilty about losing two more of the monks, but even more guilty over losing Pierce, Davis, and Brand.

She wandered listlessly toward one of the other hovercrafts, where Davis's body lay beneath a blanket. If he'd been wearing his bulkier body armor, he'd probably still be alive. While planning their mission, however, the group had decided not to risk it for the sake of the diversion. Hard to blend in with a rowdy bar crowd if you resembled law enforcement.

But perhaps it had been a mistake. Perhaps, at the very least, she should have smuggled in some more deputies.

As if sensing her inner conflict, Lady Ris touched Lilly's shoulder. "Our casualties were for a good cause."

Wiping away her tears, Lilly merely nodded. Although they had managed to reclaim the precious nans and transport them back to Trame, the mission had cost them all dearly. Even Bechet and Dreyla had lost someone they loved. And none of them were out of the woods yet. It wouldn't take long for Darkbur to mobilize his extensive forces and unleash another siege upon poor Trame. And this time, he might not leave a single structure untouched.

OK, back on the clock.

Lilly had no time to grieve or second-guess herself. She had much-needed medication to distribute.

Hastily, she assembled a task force of able-bodied

monks in the same meeting hall where this critical mission had begun.

"We should get the word out about the meds," she said. "Put it on every broad-wave signal around the planet."

"I believe it will require a combined effort of Naillik, Yerdua, and Elocin to deliver the nans quickly enough," Lady Ris said.

Lilly nodded. "The three capital towns will be easy enough, but I'm worried about the people living in the smaller villages and isolated mining operations. It might already be too late for them."

"We can take some of the nans," Lady Ris suggested, "and begin making... house calls."

Lilly almost laughed at the image. How would the grubby miners react if the gorgeous Ladies of Morbious showed up at their door to administer life-saving nano-biotics?

"I'll get word to our hospital in Naillik," Lilly said, "but I think I'll let Milo and Jacer communicate with their people."

Lady Ris's eyebrows rose, a characteristically polite form of disagreement.

"I'm not a politician," Lilly explained, "but I suspect there may be some strain between the races."

Together, Lilly and Lady Ris oversaw the transfer of

several med crates to waiting transport vehicles and the rest to a secure location beneath the monastery. As it turned out, the monks had also helpfully loaded all the trunks from their hotel rooms into the other two hover-crafts, so after unloading them as well, the time had finally come to carry the bodies of Sienna, Piper, and Davis to a sacred chamber, where they would await a proper burial.

After saying a silent goodbye to her faithful deputy, Lilly followed Lady Ris to the medical building, where Jacer, Milo, and Bechet were all awake, alert, and, of course, complaining. After tending to their injuries, the medical staff had apparently administered a special energy potion to each of them, so despite their need to heal and recover, they all wanted to join the task force.

Before entering the recovery room, Lady Ris hesitated. "I still do not understand. Why should there be any strain between the humans, dworgs, and aflins?"

"It doesn't matter that we got the meds back," Lilly reasoned. "Yerdua and Elocin will still blame the humans for stealing them in the first place."

Lady Ris gave no response, but her furrowed brow said enough.

Lilly led the way into the recovery room, where Dreyla was pushing Captain Bechet against his mattress, trying to keep him from getting up and busting open his wound.

"No," he cried, "we need to go back for Tosh!"

"Captain Bechet," Lilly said, rushing toward his bed. "*Remy...*"

He stopped struggling and looked at her, his hazel eyes burning with purpose.

"We don't know where he is," she said. "Or Brand either. We don't know if Darkbur has them, or if they managed to escape."

"Captain, that city is now a hornet's nest," Lady Ris interjected smoothly. "We have not even heard from Char and Maia, the monks that originally took Tosh in."

Remy's mouth flattened into a hard line, his gaze dropped to the floor, and his shoulders sagged. Lilly understood his dismay—oh, how she understood. Even though they had reclaimed the meds and would be able to save countless lives, she still found the losses hard to bear.

In the melancholy silence that ensued, she caught part of an argument that had erupted between Milo and Jacer, and her heart sank even further.

"Jacer received a message from his home world," Bellia said, stepping beside her. "The aflin council on Elocin has declared a state of war between them and the humans."

"But I can explain that Naillik had nothing to do with it," Jacer protested from his bed. "Once they hear we have recovered the meds, they will understand. What they do not yet realize—"

"It won't matter," Milo interjected.

"You're just being stubborn," Jacer retorted. "The message was sent before we even entered Bane. I've only just received it."

"Unfortunately, it went out on all aflin frequencies," one of the attending monks announced.

"But we have the nano-biotics," Remy insisted, who seemed to have emerged from his temporary funk.

Frowning, Milo shifted his eyes to the floor and cupped his hand over his right ear. After a moment, he pulled it away and turned back to the group.

"Oh, no," he groaned. "Yerdua has also declared war."

Lilly had removed her own comms earpiece during the journey across the desert, so she hadn't heard the bad news. Not that it would have mattered. The one she'd worn had only been tuned in to the rest of her fellow liberators. She suspected Milo had switched comms after awaking in a hospital bed.

"Look," she said staunchly, "we, the people of Vox, can get this straightened out."

Milo shook his head. "As with the aflins, this decision also came from my home world, Sheriff. Directly from the Minister of Defense herself."

"We are supposed to treat any human as an enemy,"

Jacer lamented, as if relinquishing his position that the situation could be explained and diffused.

"That's just dumb," Remy said.

"So, you two," Dreyla asked, pointing to the dworg and the aflin in turn, "are at *war* with us?"

"Don't be daft, girl," Milo growled. "We're not going along with this."

A tense moment passed as all eyes landed on the aflin. But then Jacer nodded, too.

Thank Zog for small wonders.

After what they'd just endured, their little party seemed to be intact.

Well, not fully.

Brand and Davis might have been occasional pains in the ass, but they were her people... they were her friends... and despite striving to remain detached from her colleagues, she had cared deeply for them.

Remy wiped a tear from Dreyla's face with his thumb. The small, loving gesture gave Lilly a strange sense of comfort—as if he were vicariously wiping away her own tears—the tears that, at the moment, she seemed incapable of shedding.

"What are we gonna do?" Dreyla asked.

"You will all stay here until you are well enough to travel," Lady Ris said in a maternal voice. "Longer, if you wish. We have already started shipping meds out to Naillik, Yerdua, and Elocin. Perhaps tensions will ease when the people begin receiving their nans."

The room fell nearly silent, the only sounds made by the women tending to their three recalcitrant patients.

Lilly watched as Remy further consoled Dreyla with whispers and hugs. The girl was so young—too young to deal with being stuck in the middle of a war. Then again, she possessed some serious inner strength and was smart as hell.

As if proving her point, Dreyla suddenly straightened up and wiped any lingering tears away. "Wait a second. Don't the people of Bane need the meds, too?"

Lilly sighed. "When we were divvying up the crates, I realized that a good ten percent of the nans were missing. More than likely, Darkbur's already sold them to the highest bidders of Bane. And as for the rest... yes, the people of Bane need them, too. But it's too risky for us to go back just yet."

Dreyla winced, then nodded. Hopefully, she understood that Lilly was doing the best she could.

Leaving the patients to rest, Lilly quietly slipped into the corridor. But she'd only made it halfway to the outer doors—which the diligent monks had repaired since the siege—when she heard hasty footsteps behind her.

"Sheriff Lilly!"

Turning, she spotted Dreyla hastening toward her.

Breathlessly, the girl said, "I just wanted to thank you. For helping Remy back there in the hovercraft. He might've bled to death otherwise."

Lilly smiled. "Of course."

Dreyla chuckled awkwardly. "Funny, though, since you threatened to shoot him."

Lilly blushed. "I wouldn't really have done that, you know. I just needed to get those meds as far from Bane as possible."

Dreyla nodded. "Guess it worked. He wouldn't have left Tosh behind for anyone else."

Lilly shook her head. "He didn't turn around for me. Or the planet. He did it for you. To keep you safe."

Dreyla blinked. As sharp as she was, she still possessed a teenager's naivete and temperament. Easier to blame Lilly for leaving the old doctor behind than to face her own guilt.

In an unusual moment of maternal compassion, Lilly embraced Dreyla. "Don't worry. Your old doc seems pretty resourceful. Don't give up on him yet." She stepped backward. "Now, go take care of your father before he tries to escape again. He was shot, for Zog's sake!"

Lilly smiled reassuringly, then hurried outside and ventured to Trame's communications hub. She needed to contact her remaining deputies and tell them to put Nail-lik's defenses on high alert. She had intended to warn them of Darkbur's inevitable invasion, but with a possible war on the horizon, the town had even bigger worries now.

Chapter 26

REMY

Between the pain in his gut and his restless thoughts about Tosh, Remy didn't get much sleep during his first night of recovery. By early morning, though, he felt strong enough to emerge from his sickbed. Leaving Dreyla snoozing in a nearby chair, he furtively dressed, slipped on his boots, and ventured outside in search of Sheriff Greyson.

During his initial visit to Trame, he hadn't had much time to explore the grounds and enjoy the full experience of this isolated sanctuary. Sheltered by a rocky cliff and protected by formidable walls, the monastery and its many outbuildings were the loveliest structures he'd yet seen on this arid planet.

But even more remarkable were the gardens—lush, green, and very un-Vox-like. His short time on this unappealing globe had given him the impression that the entire rock was just that... a rock. In Naillik and Bane, he'd only seen a small amount of foliage, mostly shrubs and tiny saplings. But Trame, with its blooming flowers, exotic plants, fruitful trees, gorgeous fountains, and inviting pools, boasted as much beauty and tranquility as the most vaunted paradise on Earth.

How had the Ladies of Morbious established such a wondrous haven on Vox of all places? More to the point, how did they manage to keep the foliage alive amid a scorching desert?

After wandering among the pathways for a while, he finally encountered the sheriff in a cozy flower garden. He'd recognized her from behind as she bent over a bush of oddly shaped blossoms with purple, gold, and green petals.

How appropriate. Just like Dreyla's smoke bombs.

Grinning, he cautiously approached her. He didn't want to startle her as she examined and perhaps sniffed the flowers, but he felt an overwhelming desire to speak with her.

"How the hell did the Ladies of Morbious manage to create such an oasis here in the middle of nothing?" he asked.

"There are natural springs beneath Trame," she explained, straightening up and turning to face him. Given her placid, smiling countenance, she'd obviously been aware of his presence.

"And here I thought it was magic."

Ignoring his wry comment, she said, "It's why they settled here in the first place. They felt it was a sign from Morbious herself. That, as long as they maintained their faith and hard work, this small piece of heaven would forever provide them with all the fertility necessary to sustain life."

"Fertility? I haven't seen any little ones running around here."

She chuckled. "Not that kind of fertility. More like abundance."

He glanced behind him and noticed a couple of monks tending to what looked like hibiscus bushes. The sheriff was right about one thing: The Ladies of Morbious were an industrious bunch. And despite their seemingly hedonistic way of life, they hadn't hesitated to help his team recover the nano-biotics. They'd even lost a few of their own in the process, and even more impressive, they seemed at peace with it all.

Granted, an unspoken need for revenge had likely motivated their assistance, too, but who could blame them after Darkbur's unprovoked attack on their sanctuary?

Reflecting on their losses compelled him to glance at the sheriff again. Perhaps reading his troubled mind, she let her smile melt away, and sadness again clouded her lovely eyes.

"I'm sorry about Davis and Brand..." he faltered. "They were good people. Good deputies."

She nodded. "They were... friends, too. As with a lot of my deputies. Since I lost Tim, my husband... they'd become my family, I suppose." She sighed, her expression filled with remorse. "I don't always show it like I should, but still..."

"I know the feeling," he said quietly.

She stared at him for a long moment, then asked, "How long had the doctor been with you?"

Her question sparked a memory in his mind, tugging him back to the first time he'd met the odd stranger who'd introduced himself as Dr. Robert Tosh. The day the old man had talked his way onto the *Jay*. Remy, young and ambitious at the time, had had no intention of letting him on board, but as it turned out, the doctor had offered more than just his extensive medical skills and impressive music collection. He'd also possessed an unusual, infectious quality—an unrelenting ease and enthusiasm with which he approached life.

Recalling some of Tosh's more ridiculous antics, he unleashed a hearty laugh that pained his sore stomach. "Fifteen years." Then he sobered quickly. "Not long enough."

She nodded, her eyes radiating sympathy.

"Some of the crap he pulled..." He shook his head. "You wouldn't believe it."

"Brand and Davis, too," Lilly said quietly.

A comfortable silence fell between them. Standing side by side, they both turned back to the flowers.

Suddenly, a strange notion popped into Remy's mind.

"Damn!" he exclaimed.

Startled, the sheriff widened her eyes. "What?"

"In all the craziness of the battle, I didn't get a chance to test out my grav-speakers," he said. "Really wanted to blare some B.B. King at those guys. Figured it would at least distract them a bit."

"Really, Bechet?" she asked in mock disgust.

Even after slipping a few times and calling him by his first name, it seemed her barriers hadn't fallen away completely.

He raised an eyebrow. "It's Remy," he reminded her, "and Sheriff, you ain't heard music until you heard the blues."

"It's Lilly," she conceded, a tiny smile lighting up her face. Sighing, she added, "And perhaps you'd better explain your fascination with this... blues?"

"Well, *Lilly*," he said, beaming, "it's only the best music in the galaxy, the universe... well, anywhere."

Her face still wore a puzzled expression.

Remy unbuckled the small satchel at his side and removed his tablet. As she patiently observed, he took a few moments to swipe through the menus. Finally settling on one of his favorite tunes, he tapped the selection, and a few seconds later, the song emerged from the tablet's tiny speakers.

After a moment of listening, she tentatively asked, "So, this is that B.B. King guy you mentioned?"

He shook his head. "No, this is Elmore James, singing 'The Sky Is Crying.'"

They listened for the entire three minutes of the song, both swaying a little to the music. As it wound down, Remy noticed a single tear sliding down Lilly's cheek. In a rare moment of intimacy, he gently wiped it away.

Footsteps on the path behind them announced that their private time had come to an end. Remy paused the next song in his playlist and turned to face the newcomers. Jacer and Dreyla ambled toward them, led by a limping Milo.

"Just what are you doing out of bed, Captain?" Dreyla asked him sternly.

He smirked and glanced at the dworg and the aflin. "I could ask the same of them."

"Face it, Dreyla," Lilly said. "These three are too stubborn to sit still for long."

Dreyla sighed. "You're probably right."

For a few peaceful minutes, the five of them moseyed through the gardens together, but Remy found it tough to enjoy the break. Their present tranquility wouldn't last. It was merely a fragile moment of calm before the storm.

Oddly enough, it was the aflin who interrupted their brief span of serenity.

"Sheriff," Jacer said, clearly having determined to get down to business, "Milo and I have decided to return with you to Naillik. Perhaps we can open up communications with the home worlds from there and start a dialogue about this whole mess?"

"I have no intention of going back to Yerdua just to be told I have to prepare for some stupid war," Milo concurred.

"Is it really going to come to that?" Dreyla asked, picking up a fallen bud from the path and twisting it in her fingers.

"It has before," Lilly said.

"What?" Remy asked. "When?"

"Oh, yes," Milo replied. Then, in the matter-of-fact tone of a school-aged kid reciting a history lesson, he said, "When Vox was first discovered, it was claimed by the dworgs, the aflins, and the humans."

Jacer gesticulated with sweeping movements of his spindly arms. "A planet with a new energy source that allowed us to travel faster and farther in the galaxy, not to mention power all of the cities on our home worlds. It was a treasure beyond imagination."

"So, naturally," Lilly added, "all three planets fought one another for the right to mine here." She sighed heavily. "In the end, when the war proved too costly and too deadly, they decided to share it. Signed a treaty and everything. Hence, the three main settlements—Naillik, Elocin, and Yerdua—each named after its corresponding home world."

Before Remy could probe them for more information, one of the Ladies of Morbious darted toward them.

"The controller says there is an enormous hovercraft approaching," she panted. "Whoever is driving it has been warned to keep their distance, but there has been no response."

"Where is it now?" Remy and Lilly asked in unison.

"It is not far from our front gates, but the mini-wings are set to destroy it if it turns hostile."

Remy stepped forward. "Wait, did you say an enormous hovercraft?"

"Yes. It looks like a trash hauler."

A trash hauler approaching Trame?

Remy squinted. "So, not obviously armed?"

The monk shook her head. "Not obviously, no."

Remy glanced at Dreyla, who seemed as confused as the rest of them. He felt a smile creeping across his face.

"What?" Lilly snapped.

"Come with me," he said, heading out of the gardens.

The others followed him closely—some eagerly, some rather reluctantly.

By the time they reached the front gates, the giant, metallic-blue trash hauler had stopped. From one of the guard towers, the small group could see it waiting there, about fifty yards from the main entrance of Trame. It remained still, making no move, no noise, but looking a little ominous all the same.

Despite his companions' trepidation, though, Remy felt at ease. Quickly, he jogged down to the gates and asked the armed monks to open them.

"It could be remotely run, Remy." Lilly, who'd

trailed him from the tower, gripped his bicep, trying in vain to restrain him. "Hell, it could have explosives in it... from Bane."

He arched an eyebrow. "Like a Trojan horse?"

"A what?"

He shook his head. "Never mind."

As the gates opened just enough for him to pass, Remy brushed past her toward the vehicle.

"Captain?" Dreyla called after him.

He didn't have time to answer her, though, or share his suspicions with anyone before the wide driver's-side door opened, followed by a dramatic waft of aromatic vapor, and an old man climbed out... *their* old man.

Tosh was positively beaming, with a self-satisfied grin to beat all the rest, and it wasn't due to the drugs this time.

"TOSH!" Dreyla screamed, sprinting past Remy.

A few seconds later, as she twirled around in the doctor's loving arms, Remy spotted tears sparkling on her cheeks again—only this time, they were tears of joy. Tosh, meanwhile, looked just as happy and relieved to be embracing his young crewmate.

The rest of the small group ambled toward the massive vehicle, Jacer and Milo a little slower due to their injuries.

The passenger-side door opened just then, and

Brand hopped to the sand, her disheveled blonde hair shining in the sunlight. Remy turned to Lilly, who was standing beside him, and watched an unabashed smile spread across her lips—the widest, purest, most joyous smile he'd spotted on her face since meeting her. A smile so blinding it almost hurt him to witness it.

In a flash, she darted across the sand and embraced her young deputy, whom, until this moment, Remy, along with everyone else, had believed to be dead.

"We've got injured people inside," Brand stated as she stepped out of the embrace. "Char and Maia were both shot trying to get us to safety. They need urgent help."

Remy didn't know where they'd come from, but a moment later, twenty Ladies of Morbious, Lady Ris included, appeared outside the gates of Trame. Some helped the wounded out of the vehicle while the others warmly welcomed Brand and Tosh.

Remy just lingered in place, observing the heartwarming scene. Eventually, Tosh made his way toward him, stopping about two feet away.

"Like my ride, Captain?"

"It fits you." Remy grasped the old man's hand, intending to shake it heartily.

But Tosh, being Tosh, simply pulled him into a bear hug.

Remy inadvertently winced.

"Captain, you have a lower abdomen injury."

"Nothing gets by you, Doc."

Despite the discomfort, Remy let the embrace linger a moment longer—though his joy was marred by the guilt of having left the doctor for dead.

"Sorry about leaving you behind, old man," Remy mumbled.

Tosh waved his comment away. "You had to protect Drey. That's all that mattered."

Remy smiled, somewhat relieved.

Brand's voice suddenly cut through the happy atmosphere. "Where's Davis?"

Remy threw Lilly a sympathetic look as she guided Brand away from the group to explain what had happened. Brand took the news hard, sobbing against Lilly's shoulder.

Wincing, Remy turned his attention back to Tosh, who was recounting to Dreyla how he and the women had managed to escape from Bane. Apparently, the two Ladies of Morbious had arrived at the twelfth-floor suite, looking for him, just moments before Brand had shown up. Some interference had blocked their comms, so they'd had no way of contacting the rest of the group.

Instead, they'd managed to slip out of the hotel unnoticed—easy to believe, given the mayhem all around them, not to mention Darkbur's fixation on the rear build-ing of his property—and tried to reach their hovercraft.

"Unfortunately, though," Tosh explained, "some jerkwad had gone and torched it. Maybe Darkbur's men did it after you all took off."

"They do know what our crafts look like," Lady Ris agreed.

"Course," Tosh added, "it could've just as easily been some pissed-off residents. Bane is an unholy mess right now. What happened at the Butcher's Place seems to have sparked riots all over the city."

"Couldn't have happened to a nicer place," Remy joked.

Tosh chuckled. "So, anyway, we had to find another ride. While trying to, we ran into some of Darkbur's men, which is how the ladies got injured. I managed to stop the bleeding, but we had to get out of there." He sighed. "That's when I spotted the trash hauler and figured no-body was gonna stop an old man driving a bunch of gar-bage out of the city."

Dreyla squeezed his wiry arm. "Good thinking, Doc."

"The only problem," Tosh added with a chuckle, "the piece of junk didn't have any working comms, so we were worried you might blow us the hell up before we had a chance to say *hello*."

Lady Ris cleared her throat. "Yes, well... we were about to."

"Only you, Tosh," Remy said, laughing, "would think to use a garbage truck as an escape vehicle."

In the comfortable lull that ensued, Brand finally broke away from Lilly and stepped up to Tosh. To Remy's utter amazement, she kissed the old man on the cheek, tears still trickling out of her eyes.

"Thank you for saving my life."

Tosh winked at her. "More than welcome, darlin'."

Chapter 27

LILLY

Lilly gazed through the open doorway of her office. Remy stood in the corridor, regarding a newly mounted portrait of Deputy Davis. Beneath the commemorative image, a plaque declared how the officer had bravely fought and perished to save the innocent. Lilly had arranged to have both items installed shortly after she and her companions returned from Trame. She'd even invited Davis's relatives to the unveiling ceremony, and they'd, in turn, welcomed her and his friends to a small funeral in his honor. The least she could do for a deputy who'd meant so much to her.

A week had passed since the battle in Bane, and so far, Darkbur had yet to make his move. No doubt he had a plan of retaliation in motion, but for now, he was likely busy rebuilding his business, reassembling his army, and holding off any opportunistic competitors.

Lilly and her colleagues had exhausted themselves trying to disperse the nano-biotics around the planet, even on the down-low in Bane. Although many citizens had died while awaiting the life-saving meds, she was grateful for the thousands and thousands of people who had lived, thanks to their perilous mission. Now, as she and her cohorts attempted to prepare for the probability of war, they also managed to make some time for other pertinent matters.

While Remy lingered in the hallway, Jacer and Milo sat on the opposite side of her desk, engaged in an engrossing conversation with Tosh. At least they seemed to consider it engrossing. To be fair, she'd only partially paid attention while attempting to complete an inventory of the station's weapons on her computer.

"I think I can seriously improve it," Tosh said, standing between the aflin and dworg, holding out a tablet for them to see. "And replicate it much more quickly than usual."

Apparently, the doctor believed he could not only

reproduce the nano-biotics, but also increase their potency tenfold, eliminating the need to wait for last-minute shipments from the other end of the galaxy.

"The doctor may like to partake in a bit of juice from time to time..." Remy said, stepping into the office.

She figured *juice* meant the narcotics the doctor constantly administered to himself, or whatever else gave the old man his perpetual buzz.

"...but he is one helluva doctor back in our solar system," Remy finished, looking her straight in the eye.

"I believe him," she said, leaning back in her chair, "and you, too, for that matter. I may not fully grasp the science behind what he's talking about, but I can definitely speak for everyone here when I say he has our full support."

Beaming, Tosh offered a comical half-bow and placed the tablet on her desk. With his leathery skin, innumerable wrinkles, and pale, bluish-gray eyes, he looked a little ghoulish, even when he smiled, but she found herself grinning anyway. She just couldn't help but adore the guy.

"Come on, Doctor," Jacer said as he rose from his seat, "I can introduce you to the medical staff over at the hospital."

Milo stood, too. "I'll tag along. Maybe we can use it as a bargaining chip to cool off this situation."

Communication had already collapsed between the

cities of Naillik, Elocin, and Yerdua. According to Mayor Cansen—who was way more stressed-out and red-faced these days—a breakdown of negotiations had even occurred between the dworg and aflin councils. So much for the hallowed, bilateral cooperation between the two non-human races. Stupid politics and a deplorable lack of common sense and common courtesy had fueled the flames of war.

After Tosh, Jacer, and Milo left the office, Remy sat in one of the vacated chairs. He looked a whole lot better now that his fever had passed and his wound had healed. His black, silver-flecked hair shone from a recent shower, his scraggly beard and mustache had given way to a neatly trimmed frame around his well-shaped mouth, and a mischievous twinkle had returned to his eyes. Was it possible, too, that someone—perhaps Dreyla—had laundered and ironed his favorite black-and-brown shirt, which, as usual, highlighted his lean, sculpted upper body?

He winked at her, likely realizing she'd been checking him out again.

Her eyes darted self-consciously back to her computer.

"I understand someone stole the med ship," Remy said.

While her crew had recuperated in Trame, someone had swiped the vessel from under Skully's nose. She had her suspicions, of course, but no proof.

"Yep," she said, smiling impishly. "Sorry, I know you wanted to steal it again."

"Funny. True, but funny."

"So, I was thinking..." she said, watching him closely.

"*Sheriff,*" Potter's voice interjected via the internal comms unit on her desk.

"What is it, Potter?" she snapped.

She'd been on edge ever since returning from the monastery. It didn't help that, every time she'd tried to speak with Remy, she'd gotten interrupted.

Still, she really needed to temper her short fuse. Her remaining deputies didn't deserve her ire, especially since she didn't know which one of them she might lose next.

"*You're not gonna believe who's called in to talk to you,*" Potter continued, likely old enough to ignore her outbursts, or at least not take them personally.

"Gono Darkbur," she and Remy chorused in response.

"*Uh, well... yeah,*" Potter said, with a slightly disappointed tone.

Lilly sighed. "Put him through."

A second later, her long-range comms lit up, and the crime lord's infuriatingly smug face appeared on the screen.

Without waiting for him to make the first move, she said, "You've got a lot of nerve calling here."

"Sheriff, you should calm yourself," Darkbur replied. *"Hysteria is not a good look on a woman of supposed authority."*

"Gono, you're a piece of scum," Remy shouted from off-camera. "Actually, that's giving scum a bad name. This whole crapstorm of a war is your fault!"

Lilly flashed him a stern look. She didn't need him escalating the situation.

Darkbur guffawed. *"Ah, the wayward captain. Finally found your home port. And as usual, you've picked the wrong side."*

"Not from where I stand," Remy snapped.

After another hefty guffaw, Darkbur asked, *"Haven't seen Tara Shaw lurking around, have you?"*

"The way I figure it," Remy growled, circling around to Lilly's side of the desk, "she abandoned your dumb ass, jacked a ship, and is no doubt sipping margaritas on Musk Station by now."

Darkbur waved his thick hand in dismissal. *"We'll see... anyway, Sheriff, I believe you've come to see the necessity of us working together?"*

She laughed. "This morning, I read a report that, after we took the nans back, several other factions rebelled against you. Did that bit of news not reach your mansion yet, Gono?"

"Squashed, just like your poor deputy," the crime boss sneered.

She felt heat rising from her stomach, through her throat, and up to her forehead. "The next time I see you," she spat, "you're a dead man."

"Not if one of my lieutenants gets to you first."

"I wouldn't hold out hope for that, you piece of crap."

Before he could respond, she clicked off the comms. After a few seconds of staring at the blank screen, she sank her forehead into her clasped palms.

"Shouldn't have lost my cool like that," she mumbled.

"Hell, yes, you should have," Remy replied hotly. "He'll get what's coming to him. Trust me, I've dealt with people like him before."

She peered over her intertwined fingers. "I'll bet you have."

Remy flashed her a pseudo-wounded look, then shrugged, smiled, and reclaimed his seat. "I am curious, though... what do you plan to do with Yercer? He's been in jail for two weeks now."

In fact, even now, she could hear him yelling something inane from his cell. Probably complaining about his broken wrist, which had yet to fully heal.

"He can rot in there, for all I care," Lilly said. "Until Darkbur shows his face again to claim him, or the town council decides to convict him for fraud, he's not going anywhere. No one in Naillik gives a hoot about his so-called rights. Besides, we've got bigger problems at the moment—or haven't you been listening?"

Remy offered his customary half-grin, a roguish twinkle in his eye. "Of course, I have. You've got my full attention. You always do."

Lilly blushed, then gamely recovered her composure. "So, it sounds like Tosh might be busy for a while, but after he cracks the nans dilemma, what are you and your crew going to do? Try to find your way home?"

The question had sat on the tip of her tongue for the past several days—ever since they'd returned to Naillik. It relieved her to finally get the words out, but she found herself dreading an answer she didn't want to hear.

The roguish grin faded away, and Remy's gaze turned serious. "First, I need to fix my ship," he finally admitted. "Of course, I don't think that's going to be easy. So, yes, I suppose we'll be here for a while."

"In the meantime?" she asked, striving to sound cool, disinterested.

"Well, your brother's been trying to convince me to help him out on a little job."

She raised an eyebrow to that unwelcome notion.

But Remy caught on fast. Smiling, he said, "Of course, Drey thinks that wouldn't be—"

"Why don't you come work... with me?" she asked. "Here, at the station. We need all the help we can get. And you've proven yourself to be fairly capable."

She found it hard to maintain eye contact as he ruminated on this possibility.

"Listen, I'll be around if you need help... but Dreyla would never let me live it down if I became a cop." Remy's gaze shifted to the sheriff's badge lying on her desk. "No offense."

Lilly had never heard the term *cop* before but figured it referred, rather derogatorily, to someone in law enforcement. All worlds and cultures had nicknames for those in authority.

"And as for my brother?"

"No," he said, "I think we'll make our own way." The roguish half-grin had returned. "Nate's on his own."

She sighed. "Great. All the better for him to get into even more trouble."

"But like I said," Remy added, positively squirming in his seat, "I'll be around. I mean, *we'll* be around, if you need us."

With a wink, he bolted to his feet and hastened toward the door.

"Remy," Lilly called.

Hesitating in the open doorway, he turned back to her.

Her face suddenly felt warm. No doubt she was blushing.

"Thank you," she said, "for everything you did. This—this wasn't your fight, but without you, Dreyla, and Tosh, we wouldn't have pulled it off."

He nodded. "As the good doctor is fond of saying... an enigma says *hello*."

After a few seconds of awkward silence, Remy shrugged. "Yeah, I never knew what he meant by it either." With that, he winked yet again and turned back to the corridor. "Catch you later, Sheriff Lilly," he called as he vanished around the doorframe.

Her shoulders sagging, she merely stared at the space he'd left behind—and contemplated all the mixed emotions that flooded her heart, not to mention all the questions left unanswered.

Chapter 28

REMY

An hour or so after leaving Lilly's office, Remy hopped a ride to Skully's Scrapyard. Under the blazing Naillik sun, he stepped through the front entrance of the property, nodded at some of the employees on duty, and slowly approached the *Jay* near the rear wall. As he scanned her battered hull, he simultaneously felt relief at seeing her again and dismay at her current condition. Like meeting an old friend after serving—and being crippled—in the same bloody war.

While Remy was reluctantly recuperating from his gut wound—which turned out to be worse than originally thought—Dreyla had commissioned Skully to help her with repairs on the ship. Now, as he neared the two of them standing in the shade of the open airlock, he caught snippets of their discussion, which centered around determining the best way to convert the *Jay*'s power system so it could utilize the mineral Vox7.

As Remy well knew from her frequent visits to him in the infirmary at the sheriff's station, this particular dilemma was all Dreyla thought about these days, obsessive little go-getter that she was. Since Vox7 resembled a less-developed version of their own TZ107, of which they had little supply and which didn't seem to work in this universe anyhow, she figured revamping the ship's power system would be the only way to get their baby back in the sky.

"I think you're right," Skully said. "If we can design a basic converter, we should be able to install it in her power base."

As usual, all this engineering babble sounded like Greek to Remy, but he was nonetheless overjoyed that the capable mechanic and scrapyard owner had agreed to assist Drey in bringing the *R.L. Johnson* back to life. It also comforted him that Skully seemed to accept most of Drey's theories and proposals, as he knew how much she prided herself on her technical know-how.

Of course, the *Jay* needed more than just a new

power source. In a mighty effort to bust through the starboard-side entrance and kill everyone hiding on the bridge, Darkbur's asshats had done a number on the ship's hull. Skully didn't seem too concerned, though. He did own a salvage yard, after all. He had plenty of spare parts and materials, and while Remy hated to envision his faithful girl sporting a patchwork hull, he knew that, as in most cases, functionality mattered way more than cosmetics.

"Captain," Dreyla said, noticing Remy hovering beside the open airlock, "Skully and I were just saying—"

"You don't have to tell me," Remy said, holding up his hands in a *beg-mercy* posture. "I trust you two to get my girl back in the air. I probably wouldn't understand the details anyway."

Dreyla giggled. She knew her father's limitations well.

Skully, meanwhile, simply nodded. The old mechanic clearly considered the ships he built, salvaged, or repaired his *girls*, too.

Despite the innumerable differences between him and Remy, their shared worldview was probably one of the main reasons the scrapyard owner had offered them such reasonable terms for storing the *Jay* here and helping Drey with her challenging restoration project. That, and the fact that she and Remy had promised to do some side work for him. Although they had yet to determine the specifics of such work, Remy knew his daughter would enjoy tinkering with other engines and such.

Nope, he couldn't complain. The yard would provide a safe place for the *Jay* while she was being repaired. Likewise, the *Jay* would once again be home for him, Dreyla, and Tosh. In fact, Skully had already run temporary power lines into the ship, enabling them to bring some of the more pertinent systems back online.

While they fixed and cleaned up the *Jay*, the ship would be their only residence on Vox, just as she had been in their own galaxy. She was as good a home as they could possibly hope to find on this side of that weird portal. Better, even. And she had the added advantage of lying within easy driving distance of the sheriff's station. Just in case Lilly needed him.

Skully slapped his grease-stained overalls. "OK, kids, I gotta go. We're expectin' a big load of scrap material from Bane in a few minutes. A happy bonus of your successful nans mission. Lots of tearin' down and rebuildin' goin' on over there."

Remy smirked. "Nothing goes to waste around here, huh?"

"Nope."

With his eyes twinkling, the sprightly old man

dashed down the ramp and hurried toward the front entrance of his scrapyard.

Well, at least someone's benefiting from the Bane riots.

Surveying the immediate area, Remy spotted the so-called Beast, the humongous vehicle that Darkbur's men had used to rip the side door off the defenseless *Jay*. Although he could appreciate the practicality of its mad, mishmash design—and why Skully was so damn proud of it—Remy utterly loathed the monstrous thing.

"So, you're coming inside or what?"

Shaking loose the terrible memory of that first battle with Darkbur's men, Remy scurried up the ramp and followed Dreyla to the bridge. A moment later, Tosh appeared in the doorway.

"I thought you were going to the hospital," Remy said.

"I did," Tosh replied. "Didn't take long to convince the staff. Nobody wants a repeat of what happened with the last nans shipment."

Remy nodded. "Good. With any luck, we'll all be too busy to get in any trouble." He smiled mischievously. "At least for a while." His mood turned solemn. "But I promise you two, I will get us home. One way or another."

With a glowing smile, Dreyla gestured toward the weathered consoles and bulkheads around them. "Captain, we *are* home."

Grinning in approval, Tosh stepped closer to them.

"Something's not quite right, though," Remy insisted.

"What? What's wrong?" Tosh's manic smile faded, and his blue-gray eyes bored into him. "I mean, besides most of the ship being broken?"

Remy headed toward his steering console.

"No..." Dreyla gasped. "Really?"

His face broke into a massive grin as he linked his tablet to the console, swiped the screen, and made his selection. An instant later, Robert Johnson's "I'm a Steady Rollin' Man" blared across the bridge. The rusty walls and metal decking seemed to bop along with the rhythm, reverbing like crazy.

Yes, our home has a pulse again.

He turned just in time to spot Dreyla rolling her eyes. But, as he walked back toward her and draped his arm around her shoulders, she didn't budge from the spot. Didn't even squirm like an embarrassed teenager. She just lovingly patted his chest, and together, they watched as Tosh began swaying to the old-time blues.

Follow Us

We hope you've enjoyed *The Sky Is Crying*, the third book in the *Galactic Blues* series. The adventures of Remy, Dreyla, Lilly, and Shaw (and let's not forget Doc Tosh) will continue in future books...

Until then, join the Crew by clicking the link below.

Join the D.L. Martone Newsletter
(https://dlmartone.com/follow-d-l-martone)

We know you love your freedom, so we promise not to bombard you with junk mail. We'll only notify you on occasion about new releases, giveaways, and recommendations.

Of course, if you did enjoy *The Sky Is Crying*, please consider leaving a positive review on Amazon. Thanks in advance!

About the Authors

D.L. Martone is the joint pen name of husband-wife duo Daniel and Laura Martone. Part-time residents of New Orleans and northern Michigan, the Martones travel the country in their mobile writing studio, a cozy RV dubbed *Serenity*. As you might have guessed, they're huge fans of *Firefly*, which is why they remodeled the interior of their travel trailer to resemble Captain Reynolds' beloved spaceship. Together, they enjoy writing urban fantasy, post-apoc zombie fiction, fantasy LitRPG/GameLit, cozy mysteries, and, of course, space opera.

Acknowledgments

As always, we appreciate the support from our friends, families, and fellow writers—as well as the inspiration gleaned from the amazing characters and riveting plots of *Firefly*, *Defiance*, *Dark Matter*, *The Expanse*, and *The Mandalorian*. We're so thankful such awesome sci-fi shows exist.

Of course, we couldn't have started this series—or finished this book—without the love and support of each other and our beloved kitty, Ruby Azazel.

Lastly, we're grateful to you, our fellow space-opera fans, for joining Remy and his crew on their misadventures across the multiverse.